PRIM 3

D0427773

Foxy

Foxy

BY

HELEN V. GRIFFITH

Troll Associates

A TROLL BOOK, published by Troll Associates,
Mahwah, NJ 07430

Published by arrangement with William Morrow and Company, Inc. For information address William Morrow and Company, Inc., 105 Madison Avenue, New York, New York 10016.

First Troll Printing, 1990

Printed in the United States of America.

10 9 8 7 6 5 4 3 2 1

ISBN 0-8167-1821-0

For Shirley who gave Foxy a home

Foxy

Chapter 1

At night the animals came out of the woods. The raccoons headed straight for the campground, running like humpbacked cats across the scrubby grass. The small, shy deer grazed close to the trees, raising their heads at every sound.

A black shape dragged itself from the ditch beside the road and stood wet and shivering in the moonlight. The deer's noses told them it was a dog. They snorted nervously and slipped back into the woods.

The dog had been lying in the ditch for hours, afraid to move, but hunger had driven her out into the open. She looked toward the campground, her nose twitching. Finally she began to slink across the field toward the food smells coming from the camp. Her eyes rolled wildly, and she panted with fear. She was almost too terrified to move, but starvation made her desperate.

A night bird shrieked, and the dog threw herself flat

on the ground. She seemed to wait for something to happen to her. After a while she pulled herself to her feet and continued toward the campground.

The narrow sandy lanes were lined with trailers and tents. The raccoons were already busy checking around fireplaces and under picnic tables. They scattered when the dog approached, but she ignored them. She crept from one campsite to the next, licking up any crumb she found. Although the place was alive with smells, there was not much food lying around.

Some plastic bags were hung from mangrove branches near the water's edge. A raccoon climbed up through the tangle of limbs and worked its way out to the bags. The branch bent with the animal's weight, and the raccoon slowly slid to the ground, clinging to a bag as it fell. The bag ripped open, and oranges bounced and rolled across the ground. The raccoon had attacked a loaf of bread when the dog ran up with a warning growl. The raccoon leaped aside, and the dog wolfed the bread, growling softly between gulps. A movement attracted her attention, and she looked toward the tent that she had hardly noticed in her eagerness to get at the food. Someone was watching her from the tent. A boy. A human being. An enemy. The dog dropped the bread and ran. As if she were being chased, she ran through the campground and across the field and deep into the woods, never stopping until she was out of the sight and sound and scent of man.

Chapter 2

The pelicans woke Jeff. He could hear them splash down into the bay even before it was light. He propped himself up with a pillow under his chest and watched them through the tent flap. They smashed into the water and bobbed up right away like corks. Were they really fishing? How could they see what they were after? It must be working, though, because they kept doing it.

The campground was waking up. Jeff could hear quiet voices and splashes where the boats were tied in the canal not far from his tent. Now and then an engine roared and a boat chugged out into Florida Bay.

His mother's face appeared at the tent opening. "Are you awake?" she asked.

"Who can sleep around pelicans?" asked Jeff.

"We're ready to leave," his mother said. "Sure you won't come?"

"I'm sure," Jeff said. He pulled on his swim trunks

before he crawled out of the tent and stretched. "I itch all over," he said.

"Me, too," said his mother. "Sunburn. We shouldn't have stayed out so long the first day." She looked at Jeff anxiously. "I don't like leaving you alone," she said. "What will you do?"

"Swim," said Jeff. "Explore. Wrestle an alligator. I'll be fine."

It was lighter now, and the sky was full of birds flying to their feeding grounds. One by one the boats were heading out to open water.

"Ready, Shirley?" Jeff's father called.

Jeff's mother kissed him before he could duck. "See you in a few hours," she said. She ran over to the dock and climbed down into their little outboard. Jeff's father started the motor, and they all waved to each other as the boat moved down the canal.

Jeff watched them go with mixed feelings. He really didn't know what he was going to do all day. They had just arrived, and he didn't know anybody. He would feel funny going to the pool by himself.

But he also knew he couldn't spend another day out on the water. That constant, sickening bobbing of the boat, the hot sun that you couldn't get away from, the smell of the fish they caught—that was bad enough. But there was a worse feeling out there. There were things in the water. Mean-looking little fish that just might be piranhas that could strip the flesh off your bones in seconds. Portuguese men-of-war that looked like harmless blue plastic bags floating in the water. But they had long tentacles hanging down that felt like electric shocks when you touched them. And they could still hurt you when they were dead.

The things you could see were bad enough. But what about the things you couldn't see? Things that waited deep in the water for your boat to overturn. Stingrays. Electric eels. Sharks.

His mother insisted on skin diving. He and his father had to sit on one side of the boat and lean out while his mother climbed in and out the other side. It was dangerous. Once when she climbed back in, the boat began to wobble violently. She threw herself flat on the bottom, laughing, and his father was laughing, too.

"We almost turned over," Jeff said angrily, and his father said, "Oh, well, everything in the boat floats," and they kept laughing. That's how they acted out there. And Jeff was scared to death.

His father hadn't liked it when he said he wouldn't go out with them anymore. "You'd like it if you gave yourself a chance," he said, but Jeff just shook his head.

He watched them sailing off in the little boat, his father steering and his mother pointing at things. They never even thought about what was under the water. Or if they did, they just thought it was interesting.

Jeff found a towel and soap in his parents' trailer and headed for the bathhouse. Maybe a shower would help the itching. As he passed the other campsites, he kept an eye out for any friendly-looking kids. Two boys were having a catch near the bathhouse. "Hi," Jeff said, and they answered, but they didn't ask him to play. When he came out of the shower, they were gone.

He went back to the trailer and fixed himself some cereal. It was beginning to be hot. He took his bowl outside and sat on a rock at the water's edge, scattering some birds that were picking their way along the shore. There was no sand here. All the ground was rock, which had made setting up the tent a real job. There were more comfortable things to sleep on, too.

He stared down into the water. Everything in it seemed to be alive. All the rocks had things clinging to them, and little creatures kept slithering back and forth along the bottom. It sure wasn't a place for wading.

The pelicans were still crashing into the water and popping back up, looking satisfied with themselves. Jeff watched a dark, long-necked bird duck under the water and suddenly appear a distance away. A tall, thin white heron was standing perfectly still in the shallows with its head and neck at a strange angle, staring into the water with one eye.

Jeff got up with an idea of going to the pool; but when he reached it, it already looked full, and everybody seemed to know each other. He passed the pool and entered the main building at the camp entrance. There was a store with postcards and groceries and a lot of interesting beach things, but he didn't have any money on him, so he went through to the recreation hall. It was cool and quiet there with chairs and sofas and a piano, but no people. He left the hall by the back door. A German shepherd was chained a little distance away. It stood up when it saw Jeff and wagged its tail slowly.

"Hi, boy," Jeff said, but when he approached, the dog began to bark ferociously and to pull against its chain.

"Forget it," Jeff said.

He walked out to the little road that ran past the campground toward the marshes. He was beginning to feel lonely. He had never been to Florida before, and it seemed foreign. To his parents it was like coming home. They had spent a lot of time in the keys before he was born. In fact, they had met in Key West, and Jeff was born there. They were always telling him about those days. Or partly telling him. They talked about it often to each other, too. They called that time their "before Jeff" days. He felt left out when they did that. After Jeff had been born, his father got a job in Pennsylvania, and they left the keys. This was their first trip back. Their second honeymoon, his mother kept telling people. Jeff didn't want to be on anybody's honeymoon.

The farther he walked, the wilder everything seemed. Even the leaves seemed bigger than necessary, and there were large snail shells clinging to the tree trunks. He hated to think what the snails must be like.

The woods grew thick and dark on his left, and to

the right was a tree-studded swamp with white birds perched in the branches. He tried to get a closer look, but as soon as he stepped off the road, he slipped into a ditch that was hidden in the thick grass and found himself standing in water up to his ankles. Snakes! He leaped out of the ditch and back onto the road so fast that he spooked the birds. They flapped their way farther back into the swamp, and Jeff gave up the idea of a walk. Everything was too unfriendly.

He squished back down the road to the main building, wishing he had money for a soft drink. He considered asking the woman in the store to trust him until his parents got back but decided against it. What if she said no?

A girl about Jeff's age was giving water to the German shepherd. She filled the dish and then pushed it toward the dog with a stick. The dog saw Jeff and began to bark.

"Is he vicious?" Jeff asked.

The girl turned and looked at Jeff. "No," she said as if he had asked a dumb question.

Jeff came closer. "What's his name? Can I pet him?" he asked.

"King," the girl said. "Pet him if you want."

Jeff approached King with his hand out. "Hey, King," he said.

As soon as he was in range, King began to jump all over Jeff, licking him with a big, sloppy tongue and scratching him with big, muddy paws. Jeff tried to back away; but the dog's chain became wrapped around his leg, and by the time he freed himself he was a mess.

"Thanks," he told the girl.

"That's why I feed him with a stick," she said.

Jeff tried to brush away the mud, but it just smeared.

"You wouldn't think he was so friendly," he said. "He looks mean."

"He is with animals. He's killed a few raccoons," the girl said, sounding proud.

"They got in our food last night. I saw a fox, too," he said, remembering. "A black fox."

The girl's expression told him he'd said another dumb thing. "There aren't any foxes in the keys," she said. "And I don't think there are any black foxes anywhere."

"Then what did I see?" Jeff asked.

"A raccoon," the girl said.

"I know a raccoon when I see one," Jeff said. "I saw raccoons, and then I saw something that wasn't a raccoon." He didn't tell her how scared he had been. It had taken all his nerve to look out of the tent. He was sure he would be gazing into the jaws of a hungry alligator. But when he looked, there were only hungry raccoons, and then the other animal ran up. It kept in the shadows, but he saw pointed ears and thick black fur and a long, plumy tail. The raccoons were afraid of it, and for a minute Jeff was, too. Then it turned its sharp muzzle toward him, and he saw its sick, scared eyes, and instead of being afraid, he thought: *Poor thing.*

A woman stuck her head out the door. "Amber, can you give us a hand in the store?" she asked, and went back in.

"Do you work here?" Jeff asked.

"When we're busy," the girl said. "It's my parents' campground." She left Jeff there with King. He started to pat the dog, thought better of it, and slowly headed back to the campsite to wait for his parents.

That night, before Jeff went to bed, he spread left-over food on the ground where he could see it from the tent.

"We'll have every raccoon in smelling distance right here in our laps," his father complained.

"This is for the fox," Jeff said.

"Do the raccoons know that?" his father asked.

"Maybe you could leave a little sign, 'Fox Only,'" his mother suggested.

"Good idea," Jeff said. "Do you have a pencil?"

"I don't think there are any foxes around here any-way," his father said.

"Maybe it was shipwrecked," his mother said.

"Maybe you got too much sun," his father told her. They climbed into the trailer, laughing, and Jeff could hear his mother making up more crazy reasons why a fox was in the keys. Some of the reasons made him laugh, too.

He took a couple of hot dog rolls into the tent with him in case the raccoons ate all the food before the fox came.

He knew he was going to have trouble keeping awake. After his parents had come back, they all had gone swimming in the pool, and he was really tired.

He propped himself up comfortably, but not too comfortably, and waited for the fox.

Chapter 3

The dog hid all day in the woods, coming out only now and then to drink from the ditch by the road. She was hungry. The small amount of food she had eaten the night before had not been nearly enough, but she was too afraid of people to go near the campground in daylight and too weak to hunt.

That night, as soon as the campground was fairly quiet, she headed straight for the site where the most food had been. She stopped and eyed the tent where she had seen the boy, but everything was still. She had even beaten the raccoons.

She bolted the food that was scattered on the ground and was sniffing around for more when she heard a sound from the tent. The boy was watching her again, and this time he was holding food out to her. The smell was hard to resist.

"Here, fox," the boy coaxed. "Here, foxy."

His voice calmed her and attracted her. She had

never been spoken to that way, except maybe a long time ago.

"Foxy," the boy murmured. He began to inch toward her, holding out the food, and the mood snapped. The memory vanished, and instinct took over. She fled toward the woods again, to the dark and the safety of being alone.

Chapter 4

"Guess what. It's not a fox." Jeff told Amber the next day.

He had remembered to get money this time, and he was having an orange soda at the camp store.

"I told you that," Amber said.

"You said it was a raccoon," Jeff said, "but it's a dog."

Amber looked disgusted. "How could you think a dog was a fox?"

"You'll understand when you see it," Jeff said.

"You mean you caught it?" It was the first time Amber had shown any interest since he'd met her.

"Not yet," he had to admit, "but I'm going to. I saw where it went into the woods."

"Show me." Amber headed for the door.

Jeff chugalugged the rest of his drink and followed. "I didn't say I knew where it was," he said. "Just where it disappeared."

"I bet I can find it," Amber said.

At the campsite Jeff pointed out the mangrove branches where they had tied bags of food the first night.

"Tourists always lose food the first night," said Amber disdainfully. "They don't realize how smart raccoons are at finding things to eat."

"If we hadn't done it, I would never have seen the dog," Jeff said. He was getting tired of the way she always tried to make him feel dumb.

He showed her where he had scattered food. "I tried to get it to come to me, but it ran across the field. It went into the woods right by that tree with white blossoms on it."

Amber started across the field at a run.

"Wait," Jeff called, and she stopped.

"What for?"

"Move quietly and slowly," Jeff said. "It may be watching us."

Amber made an impatient face, but she did as he asked.

When they reached the edge of the woods, she began calling, "Here, dog. Here, dog."

"It's a wild dog," Jeff said. "It won't come when you call it."

He was beginning to be sorry he'd told her about the dog. She was too reckless. She was going to mess things up.

"Dogs like me," she said.

"This dog doesn't like anybody. It's too scared."

He showed her where the dog had run into the woods. "I checked this morning. A trail goes a little way in, and then it branches into a lot of trails—raccoon trails, I guess."

"Or deer. Let's look around for hiding places," Amber said.

She pushed through the vines and creepers, peering under logs and into tangles. Jeff just watched. It wasn't his idea of how to catch a wild animal. He had intended to sit somewhere quietly where he thought the dog could see him and he could gradually gain its trust. He didn't want to chase it or to scare it any more than it already was.

"This is no good," Amber said finally. "I wonder if we could set a trap."

"No trap," Jeff said, alarmed. "I don't want the dog that bad."

"I do," Amber said. "I'd like to tame a wild dog."

"No trap," Jeff said firmly.

"Maybe we could sprinkle some kind of powder around your tent," Amber suggested, "or pour paint on the ground and then follow the footprints."

"Are you serious?"

"Well, you come up with an idea then," Amber said. "By the way, the tree you're leaning against is poisonwood."

Jeff jumped away. "Is that as bad as it sounds?"

"It can make you itch."

Jeff relaxed. "What's another itch?" he said. "I itch all over now."

"That's the no-see-ums. They bite. You see the bites, but you don't see the no-see-ums."

Jeff shook his head. What a place. Poison trees and invisible biting bugs. Why did people come here?

Chapter 5

That night Jeff's parents went to a slide show at the main building.

"You come, too," Jeff's mother said.

"I'm pretty tired," Jeff said, but he didn't fool his mother.

"Are you going to spend your whole vacation trying to catch a stray dog?" she asked.

"If I have to," Jeff said.

"Then what?" asked his father.

"Then it'll be my dog."

His father nodded. "That's what I was afraid of."

His parents walked away arm in arm.

"If you get bored, come to the show," his mother called over her shoulder.

Jeff crawled into the tent. He put some food just outside the opening and tied the tent flap back out of the way. His plan was to lure the dog close to the tent and let it see him sitting there not being a threat.

Maybe after a few nights it would begin to trust him. Maybe. If it came back at all. If he hadn't scared it too much last night. Or if they hadn't chased it away when they were tramping around in the woods. One thing, he was sure no one else had caught it. It was too wild and afraid. But he could tame it. He had seen its eyes, and more than anything else the dog looked lonely. It needed somebody who understood it, and Jeff felt that he did. Amber sure didn't. She probably thought all dogs were like King. But this dog was different. It had feelings. It was special.

Various night insects had found their way into the tent. That would have driven him crazy a few days ago, but he wanted the flap open so the dog could see him.

It was early. He might have a long wait, but he couldn't leave the tent. He was sure the dog wouldn't come near if he were sitting out in the open.

He sat looking out at the black night. It was hot and still, and he thought he caught the vibration of distant thunder. He hoped it wouldn't rain, and while he was hoping, a gust of wind shook the tent and sent some cans rattling off the picnic table. It was much cooler suddenly.

The rain started as big, scattered drops. Jeff was considering taking in some towels that had been draped on the mangroves to dry when it began to pour. *Too late now,* he thought.

He was getting wet sitting so close to the opening. Should he move back inside and give it up for tonight?

Maybe the dog wouldn't come out in the rain. Even if it did come, the food would probably be washed away. The bread was already a pulp.

Lightning lit the area for a few seconds, and Jeff was startled to see that the dog was under the picnic table. It had crept into the camp through the dark and the rain, and Jeff had never seen it. And he had thought he was being alert.

The storm seemed to be circling the camp. Lightning flickered occasionally, but it wasn't close yet. The rain had slackened.

Now that Jeff knew where the dog was, he could just make out its shape under the table. He saw it come toward the tent, moving hesitantly. Although he couldn't see its expression, he knew it was afraid of the storm. At every faint rumble of thunder the dog dropped flat to the ground.

It reached the food and, without even glancing at the tent, began to nose through the soggy mess, eating hungrily. Jeff sat perfectly still, watching, until a sudden white flash of lightning made him flinch. The thunder came immediately after, a loud, jarring crash.

For a second the dog froze, its eyes wide with terror. Then, so quickly that Jeff hardly saw it happen, it leaped into the tent.

It spun around and stared at Jeff, panting so hard that the sides of its mouth were pulled back almost in a smile. It looked strange, and Jeff wondered if it was about to have a fit.

Its glance flicked toward the tent opening and then toward Jeff, and he saw that it was going to run back outside. He couldn't let it go. Not after having it this close to him.

He and the dog both moved at the same time, the dog toward the opening, Jeff toward the dog. He threw himself on it, one arm around its neck and one under its chest. *I'm going to get chewed up,* he thought, bracing himself, but to his surprise the dog didn't even struggle.

He sat up, holding it tightly, and began to talk. "It's okay, Foxy. You're with me. Everything's okay."

Jeff crawled to the back of the tent, where it was drier, dragging Foxy with him. Thunder growled again, and the dog pushed itself closer to Jeff, hiding its face under his arm. Jeff felt such pity toward the wet, shivering animal that tears stung his eyes. He was glad nobody else was there.

It was raining hard again, and the thunder and lightning were wild. Normally Jeff was uneasy in such a storm, but tonight his only concern was Foxy. He could feel tremors run through the dog at every crash, and he talked to it constantly in a low, gentle voice that he hoped was reassuring. "You're mine now, Foxy. You're safe."

Chapter 6

He lost all track of time as he sat there whispering to the dog and stroking its wet, matted fur. He forgot everything but calming it and letting it feel that he would protect it.

His father's voice outside the tent brought him to with a jolt.

"Come sleep in the trailer," he was calling. "It's too wet out here."

Jeff dragged the dog out of the tent and followed his father up the trailer steps. The animal didn't fight, but it didn't cooperate either. It was like carrying a sack of potatoes.

At the door he hesitated. "If I come in, I'll have to bring the dog," he said.

His parents stared.

"He caught it," his mother said.

"Just our luck," his father said, lifting Foxy out of Jeff's arms.

"He's wet," Jeff warned, a little too late.

"So are you," his mother said. "You're soaked. Why didn't you get in the trailer when it began to rain?"

"I didn't want to move Foxy."

"Foxy, is it?" His father was examining the dog, looking at its teeth and in its ears and ruffling its fur.

"Doesn't he look like a fox?" Jeff asked.

"She," his father corrected him.

"A female!" his mother exclaimed. "Puppies!"

His father laughed. "Well, not right away," he said.

"Soon enough. I hope you don't think you're going to keep this dog, Jeff."

"I am," said Jeff.

"But she's sick," his mother protested. "She's been starved and mistreated, you can see that. She won't make a good pet. Look at the way she just lies there and stares at you. That's not normal."

"I don't care if it's normal or not," Jeff said.

His mother frowned. "Well, she can't sleep inside. She smells, and she must be full of fleas."

"I can't let her out," Jeff said. "She'll run away. She's not sure of me yet."

"Some pet," his father said.

Jeff didn't want to argue. He knew he was going to keep Foxy no matter what. "I'll go back out to the tent," he said. "I don't mind the wet, and Foxy's used to it."

His mother started yanking blankets and towels around. "You can't sleep out there. The water's two inches deep."

She made a bed for him on the floor and put a pile

of towels beside it. "Dry her off as much as you can, and try to make her sleep on these," she said.

"Thanks," Jeff said, smiling into his mother's disgruntled-looking face.

She punched him on the shoulder. "Spoiled brat," she said.

Jeff's father stood up and dumped Foxy on the towels. "Ah, the aroma of wet dog," he said. "It's unlike any other smell."

"I'm glad you like it. We'll all smell that way by tomorrow," his wife assured him.

Jeff thought it best not to say anything. He rubbed Foxy with a towel until she was fairly dry. She lay there as limp as a rag, watching him with serious brown eyes. He thought she was probably hungry, but if he fed her, she might have to go out later. Waking his parents in the middle of the night didn't seem like a good idea. He still wasn't sure where Foxy stood. He knew he was going to keep her, but he wasn't sure how big a fight he would have to put up.

He was very wet himself and would have liked a snack, but it seemed like the time for keeping a low profile, so he just rolled up in his blanket with one arm around Foxy. He wasn't very comfortable, but eventually he went to sleep.

Chapter 7

The next morning was overcast and chilly.

"What is this?" asked Jeff. "I thought we were in the tropics."

"This is so you'll appreciate how nice it is when it's nice," his mother told him.

"I needed a break from the sun anyway," his father said, gingerly touching his shoulder.

They were sitting on rocks on the shore, watching the action on the bay. The pelicans were as busy as ever. They didn't seem to mind sitting in ice water. Actually the water probably felt warmer than the air on a day like this, but Jeff didn't intend to find out. Nobody was in the pool, and a lot of boats were still tied up in the canal. His parents had even given up their usual excursion.

His mother was looking for fossil seashells. She found one and held it up triumphantly. "Think how long this has been lying here!" she exclaimed.

"What else could it do?" Jeff's father asked.

Foxy crouched beside Jeff, looking around anxiously. She was afraid of his parents and everything else. She flinched when the pelicans hit the water, and when a boat started up in the canal, she jumped to her feet, ready to run. Jeff grabbed her and forced her to sit. "You're all right, Foxy," he said, but she couldn't relax. Her pointed ears were straight up and revolving like periscopes.

Jeff was worried about her. She wouldn't eat, although he knew she had to be hungry.

"Do you think I should take her to a vet?" he asked.

"No, because you're not keeping her," his mother said.

Jeff let that pass. "She won't eat," he said.

"No wonder," said his mother. "She has everything wrong with her—ticks and fleas and lice and worms and everything else."

"What else is there?" Jeff asked.

"Hoof-and-mouth disease," his father contributed. "Distemper, rabies, beriberi."

"Besides that?" said Jeff.

"And she's neurotic," his mother said. "If I raise my arm, she ducks, and if I speak loudly, she almost faints. I don't want to go creeping around the house, speaking in whispers."

"It would be a nice change," his father said.

"She'll get used to us," Jeff promised.

He reached down and gave Foxy a hug. She immediately went limp and slid out of his arms. Even his mother laughed.

"She has collapsible bones," she said.

She went over and knelt beside Foxy. The dog rolled over on her back submissively.

"Poor dog," Jeff's mother said. "So thin." She began to scratch Foxy's pointed ears. "Washed and brushed, her fur would be beautiful," she said. "And this tail! Like an ostrich feather."

Foxy wagged the ostrich feather timidly. Jeff and his father smiled at each other.

"Keep it up, Foxy. You're doing fine," his father said.

"It's not dogs I don't like," his mother said defensively. "It's fleas and ticks and—"

"I know," said Jeff. "Cholera and the black plague."

"I wonder if they sell flea powder at the camp store," Jeff's mother said.

"You're in, Foxy," said his father.

They left the little beach and walked through the campground toward the store. Late mornings were usually quiet, but today's weather had kept people off the water, so there was a lot of visiting going on and different-aged kids running around. Foxy was so jumpy that Jeff was afraid she might take off. He picked her up and carried her. He felt silly walking along carrying a limp, floppy dog, but he pretended he didn't notice when people looked at him.

The store was much more crowded than usual. Amber was there, but she was so busy she didn't notice him.

They couldn't find any pet supplies, but Jeff got a length of rope to use for a leash. Outside, he set Foxy down and tied one end around her neck. He doubted that she'd ever been on a leash before and feared she might fight it, but she was so anxious not to lose him that she practically leaned against his leg as he walked. It seemed safer to keep her tied, though. If anything scared her, she wouldn't be able to dash away and be lost from him before he could stop her.

"You know, this would be a good day to go to Key West," his mother said. "We could show Jeff some of the old places."

"I wonder if it's changed much," his father said.

"Oh, I hope not," his mother said anxiously.

"After all, Shirl, it's been twelve years."

"Twelve years!"

They stood looking at each other in the way that made Jeff feel left out. He knelt and adjusted the rope around Foxy's neck. He didn't want to go to Key West with them. He didn't want to see the old places and sit there while they laughed at private jokes that they never explained.

Amber came running out of the store, yelling, "You caught it!" She must have seen them from the window.

Foxy backed away, keeping her frightened eyes on Amber.

"You're scaring her," Jeff said.

Amber looked the dog over. "She doesn't look like a fox."

"She does so. Look at her ears. Look at her muzzle. And her tail. Isn't that a foxtail?"

Amber shook her head. "I never would have mistaken her for a fox."

Jeff could see she was determined not to be convinced, so he dropped it. He introduced her to his parents and then impulsively added, "We're going to Key West for the day. Want to come?"

"I'll ask," Amber said. She jumped up and dashed into the store so abruptly that Foxy ran and cowered behind Jeff's legs.

"Lively, isn't she?" Jeff's father commented.

His mother looked annoyed. "I'd better talk to her mother," she said, following Amber into the store.

Jeff could see that she was irritated because he hadn't checked with her first. He knew he should have, but at the moment the invitation had seemed like a good idea. If he had someone with him, he wouldn't feel so lonely when his parents began talking about the "before Jeff" days. He could talk to Amber, and then he wouldn't have to hear the regret for old times in their voices, and he wouldn't feel guilty for coming along and spoiling everything.

Only now that he had asked her, he almost hoped she wouldn't be able to come. She scared Foxy. She was too noisy and quick-moving, and he didn't like her very much anyway. But when she came bouncing out of the store beside his mother, he could see that the answer was yes.

"I just have to feed King," she said.

Jeff's parents went on ahead while Jeff waited for Amber.

"Let's introduce Foxy to King," Amber suggested.

"Okay."

Jeff unsuspectingly led Foxy toward the back of the house. When she saw King, she pricked up her ears and waved her plumy tail. King stood and watched their approach without moving until they were close to him. Then with a savage snarl he lunged.

Jeff turned and ran, pulling the startled Foxy out of danger. King lunged again and again, throwing all his weight against his chain in his effort to get at Foxy.

"Stop that, King," Amber said, but she was laughing.

"You knew he would do that," Jeff accused her angrily.

"He always does. He hates animals," Amber said, still laughing. It was all Jeff could do to keep from knocking her down.

He turned his back on her and headed for the trailer. He hoped his mother and father were ready to leave. He didn't intend to wait for Amber. Being stuck with her all day would be much worse than having to listen to his parents' Key West stories.

"Wait. I'll just be a minute," Amber called, but Jeff kept walking.

Chapter 8

To Jeff's disgust Amber came running up as his father was unhitching the trailer. "Here I am, Mr. Woodward," she called, and climbed into the backseat of the car with Jeff and Foxy just as if nothing had happened. Jeff couldn't figure her out. Didn't she realize what a rotten trick she had pulled? How could she think scaring Foxy was funny? Well, it was his fault she was here, and he would just have to put up with her.

His mother looked back at them from the front seat. "All set?" she asked. "Where's Foxy?"

"Under my legs," Jeff said, and Amber snickered.

His mother hitched herself up to look over the back of the seat. "Look at that," she said. "Still scared to death. We're worried about her," she told Amber. "She won't eat."

"There's a veterinarian right down the road . . ." Amber began, but Jeff interrupted.

"She did eat," he said. "She sneaked her food when she thought nobody was looking."

"Weird," Amber said.

"I'd like to know how her mind works," Jeff's father said, starting up the car.

"She's been punished so much she's afraid to do anything, even eat. She's been treated shamefully," his mother said indignantly. She flopped back down in her seat, looking mad at the world.

They drove slowly through the campground, past the card games and horseshoe tosses and the empty swimming pool. It was still cool, and Jeff's sunburned skin made him feel even colder.

They bumped down the campground road and out onto the Overseas Highway that led to Key West.

"There's the vet. Dr. Gregg," Amber said. "Right across the highway."

Jeff didn't bother to look. He might have to be with her, but he didn't have to talk to her.

He stared out of the window and soon became absorbed in the scenery. It was strange to think that they were driving along on islands. Keys, they called them here. There were bridges between the keys—some long and some so short he hardly knew they had gone from one key to the next. All along the way people were fishing while water birds watched and argued from every available post.

"Count Dracula," he said, pointing to a black bird standing with its beak tilted upward and its wings outstretched.

His mother laughed. "That's a cormorant drying its feathers."

The water, even under a cloudy sky, was many colors—silver in some places and every possible shade of blue and green. Sometimes the road took them farther inland, and then Jeff saw exotic trees, some blossoming, some with fruit.

What a mixed-up place. You couldn't even tell what season it was. Blossoms made him think of spring; fruit, of fall. Yesterday was summer, and today it was winter. Crazy. What did his parents see to like so much?

Foxy changed her position slightly and then peered up at Jeff apprehensively. It was as if she were being very careful not to disturb anyone. Or maybe she was just trying not to be noticed. He agreed with his mother—whoever had had her before had kicked her around just for fun. You could tell she expected to be hit anytime.

"Come on up, Foxy. You must be hot down there." He pulled her up on his lap, and she gave a little yelp.

He was mad at himself for forgetting to be careful when he handled her. She had a large scrape on her belly and was probably covered with bruises, although he couldn't really see because of her fur. He suspected that she had been thrown onto the campground road from a car. He couldn't stop wondering how anyone could mistreat such a helpless, gentle dog.

"Look for signs of the old railroad," Jeff's father said, and Jeff did, although he wasn't quite sure what he was looking for.

All the way down the highway Jeff's mother kept pointing out places she remembered and bemoaning changes. "Why do they have to keep building things?" she complained.

By the time they reached Key West she was becoming resigned. "It's different," she said, "but it still feels like Key West."

She turned to Jeff. "Here's your birthplace, Jeffrey. Do you feel as if you've come home?"

"Were you born in Key West?" Amber was surprised.

"So they tell me," Jeff said.

Jeff's mother gave an excited bounce. "Oh, there's so much to see. What shall we do first?"

"Eat," said Jeff.

"I like the way this boy thinks," his father said approvingly.

Even Amber threw him a grateful glance.

"Such a waste of time," his mother grumbled, but she directed them to a place she remembered for its key lime pie. "It's a specialty of the islands," she said. "You can't leave the keys without tasting key lime pie."

"You'll hate it," Amber whispered, but Jeff ignored her.

He didn't want to leave Foxy cooped up in the car, so he let her out and tied her rope to the door handle. In the restaurant he sat where he could watch her; that wasn't such a great idea because he could see how lost she looked, and it kept him from enjoying lunch.

She sat watching the restaurant door expectantly,

and whenever it opened, she stood up, wagging her tail. When she saw it wasn't Jeff, her ears went flat to her head, and she sat down and watched the door again. Jeff had to resist the urge to run out and reassure her.

He sat through lunch, though, and even ordered key lime pie for dessert, making his mother happy by telling her how much he liked it. He wasn't sure if he really did or not, but he didn't want to have the same opinion as Amber about anything if he could help it.

"Foxy will be glad to see us," he said as they left the restaurant, but even he was surprised at her frenzied greeting. She whined and yelped and pulled against the rope to reach him. When he was close enough, she leaped up on him, and when he sat on the ground beside her, she climbed onto his lap and licked his face.

"I think she was afraid you had gone forever," his mother said.

Jeff held Foxy so that his face was out of range of her tongue. "That's the longest we've been apart since I caught her."

"I didn't know she had that much energy," his father said.

"I know," Amber agreed. "All I've ever seen her do is hide and look scared."

"She can take care of herself," Jeff said in defense of Foxy, "but she doesn't have to anymore. And nobody had better try to hurt her or scare her while I'm around."

He looked at Amber, and she looked back at him defiantly. "I'm not going to hurt your dumb dog," she said.

Jeff looked up and saw his mother watching them. She felt something wrong between them, he could tell, but she didn't say anything.

The tension hadn't reached his father at all. He was talking about a train. "It'll give Jeff an idea of what's here," he said. "Do you remember where to board it?"

"No, but let's look," his wife said, hustling everyone into the car.

Jeff noticed the sign first. "'Conch Tour Train,' is that what you want?" he asked.

Amber gave him one of her "boy, are you stupid" looks. "It's pronounced *konk,*" she said.

Jeff looked at his mother. "Is it?"

She nodded. "But don't ask me why."

Jeff's father pulled over to the curb and stopped. "Look," he said, "this ride takes an hour or two. Why don't you kids go and Shirley and I will look around a little?"

Jeff was caught off guard. He didn't want to go with Amber. He knew his parents were trying to get a little time to themselves, but he didn't care. He just didn't want to be with Amber. He tried to think of a way out.

"Amber's probably been on the train a lot," he said.

She was no help. "No, I haven't, Mr. Woodward. Anyway, I like it."

"Besides"—he tried again—"I thought you wanted to show me the old places."

"We're going to," his mother assured him.

"What about Foxy?" he asked desperately. "I can't take her on the train."

"Foxy will be fine," his mother said. "She and her fleas can sit up front with me."

"We'll see you in two hours." Jeff's father sounded impatient.

Amber was already out of the car, and Jeff couldn't think of anything else to do but get out, too. Foxy came along willingly until she saw that she wasn't going with Jeff. Then she went limp. Lifting her was like picking up a dead dog.

Jeff's father laughed. "She knows all about passive resistance."

Jeff dumped her across his mother's lap and slammed the door.

As the car drove away, Foxy gazed dolefully at him, her wet black nose making smears on the window.

"She's a weird dog," Amber said. "How could you have thought she was wild?"

"She's still wild. Without that rope she'd be gone," Jeff told her.

"You mean she'd run away?"

"Sure."

"I don't get it," Amber said. "If she doesn't like you, why do you want her?"

She was looking for an argument, not an explanation, but he found himself trying to explain anyway. "She doesn't really want to run away," he said. "She just can't help herself."

Amber looked skeptical. "How can you know that?"

"I just know," Jeff said. "She wants to belong to somebody."

"Sure," Amber said. "That's why she runs away."

"She's had a bad time," Jeff said. "She's never been able to trust anybody. Nobody's ever loved her before."

Amber snorted. "You mean, you love that mangy thing?"

She had done it again. Somehow she managed to make everything he said or did seem ridiculous, even to himself. Why did he waste his time trying to be serious with her? He couldn't wait until this day was over and he could be rid of her.

Chapter 9

The train pulled in, looking like a big toy. An old-fashioned engine pulled a string of open cars roofed over with bright awnings. Jeff was glad it was a guided tour. He wouldn't have to listen to Amber. Why did she go out of her way to be so irritating? He wondered if she had any friends. He was sure she didn't if she treated everybody the way she did him. He sat back and concentrated on the talk, pretending not to hear her comments, until she finally gave up making them.

As the Conch Train chugged through Key West, Jeff forgot about Amber for a while. This odd, foreign place was his birthplace, his native city. It seemed funny.

The old houses here were different from anything he had ever seen, built to withstand hurricanes and to provide a cool refuge from the tropical sun. Maybe part of the difference was the shrubbery. The trees had names he had never heard of—poinciana, banyan, calliandra. There were trees bearing fruit he had never tasted. Flowers he had never seen before grew in people's gardens. And the palm trees—he hadn't known there were so many kinds. Maybe he had never really looked at them before. This place had seemed like a jungle to him. Now things were beginning to sort themselves out.

For the first time he heard some of the history of the keys. About the wild Caloosa Indians who had been there first, the Spanish explorers, the settlers from the mainland, from the Bahamas and Cuba. About the pirates who had used the keys as a base, the wreckers who had salvaged cargoes from the ships that went aground on the uncharted coral reefs, the fishermen, and the homesteaders. And he felt like part of it. The voice on the loudspeaker said that native Key Westers were called conchs. Was he a conch? He found himself liking the idea.

He realized how his thoughts were running and had to smile. He wasn't a real Key Wester. His parents were both from up North, and his roots were there and in the countries their families had come from. Yet . . . he had been born in Key West. No matter where the rest of his family had come from, he was from Key West.

The ride was over too soon. Jeff wanted to hear more; but he had to leave the train, and he couldn't even think over what he had heard with Amber standing there. She hadn't been affected the way he was at all. Of course, she was used to the keys. He wondered if she had any idea how strange they were to him.

"Have you ever been North?" he asked her.

"I've been to Miami," Amber said.

"I mean North North. Where it snows."

Amber shook her head. "My parents are tied to the campground. We never go anywhere."

"Then this is all you know," Jeff said.

Amber bristled. "I can read. I've seen movies. I know about other places."

Jeff walked to a bench and sat down. There wasn't any use trying to talk to her. She took everything the wrong way.

The car pulled up, and Amber and Jeff hopped in. Before Jeff was settled, Foxy scrambled over the back of the seat and into his lap.

"Is it something we said?" his father asked her.

His mother brushed at the front of her windbreaker. "I hate dog hair," she said.

"I'll train her not to shed," Jeff promised.

"That'll be nice," said his mother. "How was the ride?"

"Great." He would have liked to say more. He thought he would like to tell his mother about what he had felt while he listened to the Key West history, but he knew he couldn't in front of Amber. Or in front of his father. He wasn't even sure he could tell his mother. Spoken out loud, it would probably sound silly.

Jeff's father waited outside with Foxy while the rest of them visited the aquarium. Jeff's mother wanted to show him what it was she found so interesting under the water. She dragged him from one exhibit to another, speaking of the fish as if they were pets.

"Isn't that one adorable?" she kept saying, and: "Look how cute." She made him admire the parrot fish. "Did you ever see such colors?"

"Only on a parrot," Jeff said.

"See what you're missing?" his mother said. "It's another world down there."

That was the trouble. It was a different, alien world, and the thought of entering it made him shiver. But the fish were fascinating. More fascinating than he had thought. He stood before a tank where a barracuda slunk through waving reeds like a stalking tiger. It gave him the creeps. He pulled his gaze away, and his eyes met Amber's.

"Are you afraid to dive?" she asked.

"No," Jeff lied.

"Then why don't you?" she persisted. "I'll take you tomorrow."

"Let's go to the Turtle Kraals," his mother said quickly, and Jeff knew she was saving him from having to answer. As if he had to be protected from Amber. He was mad at his mother for thinking that and relieved at the same time.

At the Turtle Kraals his mother decided to wait outside with Foxy. "I feel sorry for the turtles," she explained.

"What about the fish?" Jeff asked.

She thought about it. "They seem more satisfied."

The turtles did seem discontented, but Jeff couldn't

be sure. Maybe it was their natural expression, the way fish always looked inquisitive and porpoises always looked friendly.

Jeff leaned against the rail, watching a big loggerhead turtle chomping on a piece of meat.

"'Once common in the keys,'" he read. "I saw that a lot in the aquarium, too. Why do people come here and kill things off?"

His father shrugged. "They're just supplying a market."

"Well, why don't they quit when something gets scarce?" Jeff asked resentfully.

"Maybe they don't know how else to earn a living," his father said. "Anyway, it's not all hunters. There are lots of reasons why a species declines."

"My father told me hunters almost killed off all the egrets," Amber said.

"Egrets?" Jeff asked. "Are they good to eat?"

Amber gave him that look. "Plume hunters. They wanted their feathers."

"For ladies' hats," his father added.

Ladies' hats? It sounded crazy, but Amber and his father seemed perfectly serious.

"They killed the first ranger that came to stop the hunting," Amber said.

"Killed him!" Jeff couldn't believe it.

Amber nodded. "Shot him."

"Don't look like that," his father said. "It was a long time ago."

There was a man at the Turtle Kraals selling conch

shells that he had made into horns by sawing off the tops. He blew into one, producing a haunting island sound that Jeff liked. He picked out a shell and paid for it.

"Let me blow it," Amber demanded, snatching it from his hands.

She tried it several times, but no sound came out.

"You were gypped," she said, shoving it back at him.

Jeff put the shell to his mouth and forced out a long, mellow tone. He and the conch-shell man grinned at each other, and Amber flounced away without a word.

They rejoined his mother and Foxy and strolled along the street, looking for souvenirs in the little shops. His mother was attracted by a display of macramé. "Look," she said, holding up a collar and leash of knotted twine. "For Foxy."

Jeff looked them over. The collar was fancy with blue beads worked into the design. It was a little stretchy, but it seemed to be strong enough. He put it on Foxy before he took off the rope, just to be safe.

"I like your outfit," his father said.

"Let's walk down to the Hemingway House," Jeff's mother suggested.

"What's there?" Jeff asked.

"Cats," Amber said.

"Cats?"

"About a hundred."

"It was the home of a famous writer," Jeff's mother said. "Haven't you ever heard of Ernest Hemingway?"

"What about the cats?" Jeff asked.

"Well, there are cats, but I don't think there are a hundred."

"It seemed like it," Amber said.

"This sounds like your kind of place, Foxy," Jeff said.

As they walked, Foxy kept as far from the street as possible, jumping skittishly when cars went by. At intersections Jeff had to jerk on the leash to make her move. Then she would rush across, head down, ears flat, and bushy tail almost trailing on the ground. She seemed to be trying to make herself as small as possible.

"See how afraid she is of cars?" his mother said. "I just know she was thrown from one."

The Hemingway House looked interesting with wide, shady porches on two levels and a garden full of palm trees.

The plan had been for Jeff's father to stay outside with Foxy, but Amber grabbed the leash before Jeff realized what she was doing.

"I'll wait here with her," she said.

"No," Jeff said. He couldn't let her stay with Foxy. He didn't trust her.

"We can't let you do that, Amber," his mother protested.

"I want to. I've seen the house anyway."

"I'll wait with Foxy," Jeff said. He reached for the leash, but Amber wouldn't let go. He knew he could get it away from her, but he hesitated. He didn't like to make a public fuss.

"We're blocking traffic," Jeff's father said, pushing Jeff and his mother through the entrance. "Thanks, Amber."

Jeff let himself be pushed. After all, they wouldn't be gone long. They wouldn't be far away. And why would Amber want to hurt Foxy anyway? But he didn't trust her. He couldn't help it. He just didn't trust her.

She was right about the cats. There were an awful lot of them. Another time he would have enjoyed looking at them all and seeing Hemingway's home, but now he was too uneasy. He couldn't wait to get back to Foxy.

As they toured the house, Jeff kept looking out the windows for a glimpse of Amber and Foxy, but he couldn't locate them.

His father laughed at him. "Mother hen," he said.

But nobody laughed when they left the house. Amber was waiting for them with a woebegone expression on her face. And she was alone. Foxy was gone.

Chapter 10

"Where's Foxy?" Jeff's mother sounded apprehensive.

Jeff couldn't speak. He felt numb with dread. Why hadn't he listened to the warning in his head? Something bad had happened, he was sure.

Amber looked from one worried face to the other. Then to Jeff's amazement she laughed.

"It's just a joke," she said.

"What do you mean, a joke?" Jeff's father demanded, but Jeff didn't give Amber a chance to answer.

"Where's Foxy?" he shouted into her face. "Where's Foxy?"

Amber backed away, looking startled and a little scared. "She's okay. Come look," she said.

She turned and ran, and Jeff ran after her. As they rounded the corner, he saw Foxy tied to a pole halfway down the block. She was fighting against the leash, straining desperately to get away. When she saw Jeff and Amber bearing down on her, she struggled harder.

Jeff stopped running. "Wait. You're scaring her," he called, but Amber kept going. Foxy gave her a wild glance and twisted frantically away from the pole. Suddenly the collar slipped over her head, and she was free.

"Foxy!" Jeff yelled, but she gave no sign of hearing him. She took off down the street with Amber in pursuit. Jeff began running then, but even as he ran, he felt that Foxy was gone. He knew how fast she was, and panic would make her run even faster. He caught up with Amber and grabbed her arm.

"Don't chase her anymore," he said.

Amber tried to pull away, but he dug his fingers into her arm.

"Don't chase her," he said.

His parents ran up, and Amber turned to them.

"I was just kidding around," she said.

Nobody answered her. They were watching Foxy. As she raced toward the intersection, Jeff braced himself for the screech of brakes and a thud. There was a lot of traffic, and he didn't see how she could possibly make it across the street.

But instead of running blindly out as he had expeted, Foxy slid to a stop at the curb. She looked anxiously around, then ran back and forth along the curb, obviously terrified and confused.

"Stay right there," Jeff commanded Amber. He started down the block toward Foxy, running when she was looking toward the street, forcing himself to walk when she turned her head in his direction.

He couldn't tell if she knew he was after her or not. There was no sign of recognition in her face when she looked at him. Her mouth was drawn back the way it had been during the storm, and she looked ready to die of fright.

As Jeff got close, he began to walk in slow motion. He was even afraid to say her name. He waited for a break in the traffic in case she got away from him and ran into the street. Then he made a grab for her.

It was easier than he had expected. She was in such a hysterical state that he was half-afraid she would snap at him, but when his hands touched her, she rolled her eyes toward him and just gave up.

He put his arms around her and buried his face in the thick ruff of fur at her neck. She was panting so hard that her whole body shook. "Hey, Foxy," he whispered.

He heard Amber ask, "Is she okay?" and he stood up. Foxy leaned against his leg, panting and quivering.

His mother had taken the new leash from the pole, and she slipped the collar over Foxy's ears. Then she leaned down and kissed her on the muzzle.

"Yuk," Amber said.

Jeff waited for his mother to say something. He knew what he would have to listen to if he did anything like what Amber had just done. But his mother just gave Amber a thoughtful look and let it go at that.

His father didn't mention Amber's trick either. "It's getting late," was all he said. "Let's see what else we can fit in before we have to leave."

Amber walked beside Jeff as they retraced their steps. "It wasn't my fault," she said. "Her collar was too loose."

Jeff looked her in the face. He felt like telling her what he thought of her and her stupid excuses and her unfunny jokes that were meant to hurt people. The words were there, all ready to spill out of his mouth. But then the same feeling that must have stopped his parents from speaking out came over him. What was the use? What difference would it make? When their vacation was over, he would never see her again anyway. She was only a temporary annoyance. Soon she would be out of his life for good.

Chapter 11

Everyone was upset and uncomfortable, and it made them all quiet for a while; but when they began driving around the island, things were better. Jeff's parents pointed out places where they had lived during their "before Jeff" and "right after Jeff" days. They drove by the beach where they had met and argued amiably about the exact location. They talked about old friends and wondered if any were still in the keys.

"I hope not," Jeff's father said. "They'd probably ask us for a loan."

Their stories were more interesting to Jeff now that he could actually see the places they were talking about. Even though a lot of their conversation consisted of "Remember. . . ?" and laughter, Jeff didn't mind. In fact, when they laughed, it made him want to laugh, too.

Amber was being quiet. She looked at everything;

but she didn't ask any questions or enter into the conversation, and that was fine with Jeff.

He had heard some of his parents' stories so often that he almost thought he remembered them himself. He pointed to a man with long blond hair who was selling coconuts decorated to look like heads. "That looks like the man you told me about who stole the turtle," he said.

His mother giggled. "You know, he does."

"If it is, he probably stole those coconuts," Jeff's father said, and his mother giggled again.

Foxy was on the seat as close to Jeff as she could get. He pulled her to the window. "Look out and see where your family used to live," he said.

"Have you noticed how Foxy acts when she's spoken to?" his mother asked.

"I know," Jeff said. "She ducks her head and kind of squints her eyes."

"She looks as if she's expecting somebody to smack her one," his father said.

"I think it's more force of habit," said his mother. "She must know by now that Jeff won't hit her."

"Do you know that, Foxy?" Jeff asked, giving the dog a rough hug.

When he let her go, she leaned against him and sighed.

"We probably should think about leaving," Jeff's father said. "Or should we eat first?"

"Let's eat," Jeff's mother said. "We'll go to one of

those fancy restaurants we couldn't afford when we lived here."

"We still can't afford them," his father said, but he drove around until they found one of the places Jeff's mother remembered.

They left Foxy in the car, staring at them through the window with her ears pointed straight up in the air.

"Now, Foxy, I'm trusting you," Jeff's mother said.

The restaurant wasn't all that fancy.

"If you couldn't afford this," Jeff said, "you must have been in bad shape."

"You've got the picture," his father agreed.

Jeff studied the menu. "Do we have to order key lime pie this time?" he asked.

"You may order from any region you choose," his mother said grandly.

"Okay, I'll have Swedish meatballs and baked Alaska," Jeff said.

His father took up the theme. "I'll have London broil and Boston cream pie."

Even Amber got into the act. "I'll have an English muffin, and—and Danish pastry," she said.

Jeff's mother laughed. "It's not that you're funny," she assured them. "I'm so tired I'm slaphappy."

Service was slow, but it didn't matter. They were all feeling weary and a little silly. Soon they were at the point where they giggled at everything that was said.

"I don't know why I'm laughing," Jeff's mother said.

"I know when we leave, we'll find that Foxy has torn the upholstery to shreds."

"Or messed all over the seats," Jeff said.

His mother reached over and patted his hand. "You're always such a comfort to me, Jeff," she said.

When they were finished, she asked for a doggy bag. "Why do they look at me as if I don't have a dog?" she complained.

"This is the first time you've asked for a doggy bag when you did have a dog," Jeff reminded her.

Foxy began bouncing up and down when she saw them coming. She was delighted to see Jeff, but not frantic the way she had been at lunchtime.

"I think she knows now that I'll come back," Jeff said.

"And look," his father said, "the car is just the way we left it."

"Except for a two-inch layer of hair on the seats," Jeff's mother said.

Jeff's father shook his head. "There's no satisfying this woman."

In the car Amber tried to make Foxy sit beside her. She pulled her close, and as long as she held her, Foxy stayed. When she relaxed, though, Foxy got up and flopped against Jeff. Amber hauled her back across the seat and tried again, but the same thing happened. Jeff was ready to tell her to leave the dog alone, but Amber gave up then. She slid down on the seat and closed her eyes.

There was very little talking on the way home. The long day had caught up with them all.

"Want me to drive, Harry?" Jeff's mother asked politely.

"I'm okay."

"Thank heaven." She sighed.

It grew dark as they drove, and the trees and bushes along the road merged into a long, irregular black hedge. Foxy arranged as much of herself as she could onto Jeff's lap and seemed to sleep, although every time Jeff moved her ears went up.

Reflections of lights from the bridges they crossed wavered in the water. There was no moon, and after a while the rain that had threatened to fall all day began to patter and then to stream across the windshield.

"Looks as if you'll sleep in the trailer again tonight, Jeff," his mother said.

His father took a quick glance over his shoulder. "They're all asleep back there."

Jeff wanted to say, "No, I'm not," but it took too much effort. His eyes kept closing, and finally he didn't force them open anymore. His head fell back against the seat, and scenes of Key West slid across his mind.

He must have dozed off because his father's voice saying, "We're home, gang," made him jump.

He forced his eyes open and saw that they were almost at the campground road. His mother turned to him, smiling, and had started to speak when his father said in a strange, sharp voice, "What's that car doing?" Before Jeff could look or even think, there was a crash that seemed to go on and on until darkness filled his brain and he didn't hear or know anything at all.

Chapter 12

Amber had never hurt so much in her life. She wanted to yell, but when she tried, only a little moan came out. Someone was talking to her, but she couldn't seem to grasp what he wanted.

She rolled her head over to look at Jeff; but his door was open, and he was gone. Foxy was gone, too.

Jeff's parents were being helped out of the front seat, and Amber finally understood that she was supposed to get out, too. She was almost afraid to try to move. What if she couldn't? But everything worked. She hurt all over, but everything worked.

"Where's Jeff?" she asked the man who was helping her.

"Take it easy now," he said, ignoring the question.

She tried again, keeping her voice calm so he would tell her the truth. "The boy who was with me. Where is he?"

"Don't worry," the man said. "I'm sure he'll be fine."

It wasn't an answer, and Amber began to be afraid. She took a deep breath to keep her voice steady. "There was a dog with us. A little black dog. Have you seen her?"

The man looked at her pityingly. "Was that your dog, honey?"

Amber couldn't ask anything else. The man led her to an ambulance and helped her climb inside.

"Just wait here a few minutes," he said kindly, and he hurried away.

Amber stared numbly out through the open back door of the ambulance. Headlights and flashlights cut through the rainy darkness, and the red light on top of a police car flashed around and around. Someone was directing lines of slowly moving traffic.

Where had everyone come from so fast? She wondered if she had been unconscious.

Flares outlined the Woodwards' car where it seemed to sprawl halfway across the highway. Amber felt a shock when she looked at the car. The front was smashed, the tires knocked crooked, the windshield cracked. How could anyone have lived through that? She had seen the car hit them. She had been half-asleep when Jeff's father's exclamation alerted her, and she had opened her eyes in time to see the car coming straight toward them. And into them.

A feeling of disbelief surged through her. This couldn't really be happening.

Two men expertly maneuvered a stretcher into the ambulance. Jeff lay on it, perfectly still, his eyes closed, his face covered with dirt and blood. For a frightening moment Amber thought that he was dead. But he was breathing. Short, shallow breaths, but they meant he was alive.

Jeff's parents were helped into the ambulance, and another man climbed in, holding a blood-soaked cloth against his nose.

"It wasn't my fault," he said.

They took off, siren screaming.

"A dog ran right out in front of me," the man said.

Mr. Woodward leaned over Jeff, gently brushing dirt from his face and hair. "Wake up," he kept saying. "Wake up, Jeff."

Mrs. Woodward seemed dazed. "Are you all right, Amber?" she asked vaguely.

Amber nodded. "I think so."

"Jeff was thrown out," Mrs. Woodward said. "He's—" Her voice thickened.

Amber just looked at her. She wanted to speak, but she didn't know what to say.

"It wasn't my fault," the other driver began again, and suddenly Amber hated him with all her soul.

"Shut up, you drunk," she said viciously.

"Shhhh." Mrs. Woodward put her arm around Amber and pulled her close.

They sat watching Jeff, and unexpectedly he opened his eyes.

"Well, hello," Mr. Woodward said in a shaky voice. "Where've you been, boy?"

Jeff looked around as much as he could without

moving his head. Amber knew what he was looking for. She hoped he wouldn't ask, but he did.

"Where's Foxy?"

There was a pause—too long a pause. Then Mr. Woodward said, "She's all right. Don't worry about Foxy."

"But where is she?" Jeff's voice was sharp with apprehension.

"She's with my parents," Amber said quickly.

Jeff looked at her.

"Really," Amber said.

They reached the hospital then, and there was no more chance to talk. Jeff was rolled away somewhere, and Mr. and Mrs. Woodward were taken away, too.

Amber was still numb. The questions and examinations seemed to be happening to someone else. Her muscles were sore, but the pain seemed to be someone else's pain.

Then her parents burst into the room, and when Amber saw them, feeling returned with a rush.

"Make them tell you about Jeff," she said. "He's hurt, and they won't tell me how bad. And Foxy," she said, beginning to cry at last. "Oh, Mom, Foxy's dead."

Chapter 13

Amber cried all the way home. She couldn't seem to get control of herself. Her father said she was hysterical, but she didn't feel hysterical. It was just that she kept seeing Jeff on the stretcher and thinking of how much he liked Foxy and how he protected her and how she trusted him. Now Foxy was dead, and maybe Jeff was, too, for all she knew. At the hospital they said his condition was satisfactory. He hadn't looked satisfactory. And what would happen when they told him about Foxy? Every time she thought of that she started to cry all over again.

Her mother tried to comfort her, but she didn't understand. She thought Amber was crying from fright or shock. She couldn't know. She had never seen Jeff and Foxy together.

A thought struck her. It took a couple of tries, but she was finally able to ask, "What did they do with Foxy?"

"I don't know, Amber," her mother said. "Try not to think about it."

"What if she's still there?" Amber pictured Foxy lying on the wet road, maybe being run over again and again. She clutched her father's arm. "Daddy, we've got to get her."

"Take it easy," her father said. "If she's there, we'll get her."

When they reached the campground road, they saw that the cars had been taken away. There was no sign that an accident had happened there that night. And there was no dog lying on the road.

"Stop anyway," Amber begged. "I want to look around."

Her father pulled over and stopped. "I'll look. You stay here," he said.

He got out of the car, and after a minute Amber did, too. She watched her father shine his flashlight into the tall grass along the shoulder of the road. The rain had stopped, but the grass stems were covered with droplets that glittered briefly as the light passed across them. Night creatures scurried or hopped deeper into the grass as Amber's father walked along the shoulder. Then the light touched a small, motionless black mound, and Amber cried out. Her father swung around.

"Get back in the car," he said roughly.

He watched to see that she obeyed him before he opened the car trunk. Then he went back to the sodden mound lying in the grass and took it up in his arms.

"He'll ruin his clothes," Amber's mother complained.

Amber couldn't look anymore. She turned her head and stared into the night, tears streaming from her wide-open eyes.

Her father slammed the trunk shut and got back into the car.

"Don't cry for Foxy," he said. "She never felt a thing."

Chapter 14

It was very late when Amber finally went to bed. She slept, but even asleep, she knew something bad had happened.

She was sorry to see how early it was when she woke up, but she wasn't able to make herself go back to sleep. Her mind was too full.

With difficulty she dragged herself out of bed. Every muscle in her body was sore. It was hard to believe that one second of impact could have such results. It hurt to move, but she was too restless to be still. She dressed and quietly slipped outside.

King leaped toward her and barked a greeting. When he had gone as far as his chain would allow him, Amber reached out and patted his huge head. It would be a comfort to hug him, she thought, the way she used to hug her stuffed animals when she felt unhappy. But you couldn't hug King. He overreacted and climbed all over you.

She walked down to the narrow strip of beach and looked out at the water and sky. The storm had blown away, and the sun was quickly drying things out.

The pelicans were fishing as usual, and the great white heron was standing in its favorite place in the shallows. A cormorant stood on a post, drying its wings, and Amber recalled how Jeff had said it looked like Dracula when it did that. It hurt her now to remember.

She wished she had been nicer to Jeff. But the way he considered Foxy his private property had made her mad. After all, it was her parents' campground. Didn't that mean Foxy should be her dog if she wanted her? Jeff didn't feel that way. And Foxy didn't either. Amber had even been mad at Foxy for preferring Jeff. It seemed silly now. Unimportant.

She walked down the road to the Woodwards' campsite. The empty tent and trailer looked sad. Amber wondered what Jeff's family would do now. How would they get the trailer home? What a vacation. They had probably looked forward to it for a long time, and then this had happened.

She had never thought of any campers that way before. Not like real people with real lives. She played with the kids sometimes, but mostly just to show off her swimming and skin diving. She didn't like them. Why should they get to go everywhere they wanted, while she was stuck here year after year?

She sat on the picnic bench to rest her aching muscles. If she felt like this, what must the Woodwards be feeling? She wished there were something she could do for them. She looked around the campsite.

Jeff's tent. With all the rain everything in it would be damp, if not actually wet. Amber crawled inside the tent and felt Jeff's sleeping bag. It was fairly dry, but there were muddy marks across it. A raccoon probably. Raccons got into everything.

She decided to air the tent's contents and began piling everything on the sleeping bag. There wasn't much there. A few clothes. A flashlight. Towels. She grabbed Jeff's pillow and was surprised to feel that it was soaking wet. She looked for a leak in the tent roof above it but couldn't see one.

She pulled everything out of the tent and spread the articles on top of the picnic table. She brushed the mud off the sleeping bag and picked up the pillow to shake it. That was when she noticed the smears of blood. And the hairs. The pillow was covered with long black hairs.

Amber stared at the pillow. They were raccoon hairs, of course. They had to be. Why couldn't she believe it?

Foxy was dead, Amber knew that. Her body was in the car trunk. But at the same time Amber knew that sometime during the night Foxy had come looking for Jeff. She had crawled into his tent, wet and bleeding, and lain on his pillow, waiting for him to come back. But Jeff hadn't come back.

Amber stood in the sunlight, shivering all over. Where was Foxy now?

With a start she realized that her father was calling her name. "I've been looking for you," he said. "Are you all right?"

Amber nodded. She didn't know how to tell him what she had just found. She wasn't sure herself.

"I buried Foxy," her father said gently.

"I wanted to be there," Amber said.

"You wouldn't have wanted to see her. She was pretty messed up."

He put his arm around her and started walking her toward the house. "I called the hospital," he said.

Amber couldn't ask anything. She just waited.

"Jeff will be all right," her father told her. "He was lucky."

"He won't feel lucky when he hears about Foxy," Amber said.

"He has more to worry about than a dog. His mother's hurt. Internally."

"Is that serious?"

"It could be."

"She was nice to me," Amber said. She thought how Mrs. Woodward had laughed at their silly jokes at the restaurant. But she didn't cry. She felt all cried out.

"When I think of you in that wreck . . ." Her father shook his head. "I'll be calling the hospital again later. I'll tell Jeff about Foxy."

"No, don't tell him yet," Amber said.

"He has to know sometime."

"Not yet," Amber pleaded.

"Well," her father said noncommittally. He pulled

something from his pocket and held it up. "He'll have this to remember her by."

"What is it?"

"Foxy's collar," her father said. "I took it off before I buried her."

Amber took it from him and turned it over in her hands. Jeff would be glad to have it, she supposed. But something was wrong. What was it?

As she stared frowning at the collar, a memory surfaced—a memory of Jeff's mother buying a collar for Foxy in one of the Key West stores. A macramé collar with blue beads. They all had said how cute Foxy looked.

But the collar she was holding now wasn't macramé. It was an old, worn brown leather strap. It wasn't Foxy's collar at all.

Amber could hardly keep from shouting. Her feeling had been right! Foxy had been in the tent. Not a ghost Foxy, but a real live, lonely, scared dog.

Hiding her excitement, she put the collar in her jeans pocket.

"Promise you won't tell Jeff anything," she said. "When the time comes, I'll tell him myself."

Chapter 15

Amber couldn't wait to get by herself. Foxy was alive, and she was the only one who knew. She had to decide what she was going to do about it.

The family ate breakfast together that morning; that was unusual. Amber supposed it was because of last night, but she would just as soon have been alone. She was used to it anyway, and today she wanted to think.

"How are you feeling, Amber?" her mother asked for what seemed like the tenth time.

"Stiff, that's all," Amber said.

"You'd better stay home from school for a few days," her mother told her. "I'd like to keep an eye on you."

Good. Now that she knew Foxy was out there somewhere, she didn't want to be away from the campground for a minute.

As soon as she could, Amber left the house and went back to Jeff's campsite. She sat at the picnic table, looking at the damp pillow and wondering.

Was it true? Had Foxy really been here last night? Or had she just talked herself into believing it because she wanted it so much? The black hairs could have been from a raccoon after all. But the collar. That wasn't Foxy's. The dog her father buried couldn't have been Foxy.

The other driver really had swerved to avoid a dog, Amber decided. But he had hit it anyway, or else Mr. Woodward had. The dog's owner would never know what happened to it. Maybe that was just as well.

Foxy must have hidden in the woods when daylight came and the camp woke up. She was too afraid of people to hang around the tent all day. But she would come back tonight. Amber was sure of it. Even if she had given up on Jeff, hunger would send her back to the camp.

Amber would put food around the tent. In it, too. She would wait until Foxy went inside and then grab her. Foxy wouldn't fight. She wasn't that kind of dog. And after she caught her, Amber would take her home and keep her until Jeff got out of the hospital.

She looked around the campsite. Where should she hide tonight? In the tent? No, Foxy might see her or smell her and run before Amber could get her hands on her. And she might not come back anymore. Amber had the feeling that tonight was her only chance to get Foxy. She had to do it right the first time.

Hiding in the mangroves wasn't a good idea either. There might be other things hiding in there with her.

Behind the trailer. That should work. It was close to the tent, and Amber could stand behind it and still see what was happening. She wouldn't be completely concealed, but if she remembered not to move, she would be just another shadow.

She felt the things she had laid out on the picnic table and found that everything but the pillow was dry. She left it out in the sun and returned the other articles to the tent, spreading out the sleeping bag and tucking Jeff's clothes inside it. Then she had second thoughts about the pillow. She crawled out and got it and put it on the sleeping bag. There. Now things looked the way they had last night. She didn't want to do anything to make Foxy suspicious and scare her off.

It seemed like a long time until night. Amber wandered restlessly down to the water, then back through the campsite and across the field to the woods that bordered the campground. She skirted the edge, searching the tangles for some sign of Foxy. She was sure she was there somewhere, maybe even watching her. There was really no use looking, though. Foxy was afraid of her. Even if she found her, Foxy would run, and Amber could never catch her in the woods.

"Foxy. Here, Fox," she called, but she didn't expect anything to happen, and nothing did.

It would be fun when she had Foxy all to herself. She would be so good to her that maybe she would come to love Amber best. Then, when Jeff came back, Foxy wouldn't want him anymore. Amber pictured the dog hiding behind her legs when Jeff tried to pet her. "Don't be afraid, Foxy. It's only Jeff," she would say. She smiled, thinking about it.

But that wouldn't happen. It would take days, weeks maybe, for Foxy to forget Jeff. He would be out of the hospital before then.

If only he wouldn't come back. If only he would go straight from the hospital to wherever he came from. But he wouldn't. He would come back for Foxy.

Amber began to wish she hadn't told him last night that Foxy was still alive. She had felt sorry for him, but why should she? His parents had a trailer; they went on trips; they even let Jeff take off from school to go along. He could probably have anything he wanted, including any dog.

All Amber had was that crazy King, and he wasn't really hers. Anyway, he was a watchdog, not a pet. Amber wanted Foxy. She wanted to take care of her. She wanted Foxy to look at her the way she looked at Jeff.

Amber turned suddenly and hurried back to the house. She found her father in the office.

"Have you called the hospital yet?" she asked.

"Not yet."

"Well, when you do," Amber said, "tell Jeff about Foxy. That she's dead. He might as well know that she's dead."

Chapter 16

Amber hid behind the trailer and worried. The longer she waited for Foxy to appear, the dumber her plan seemed. It was dark, but it wasn't late. People were wandering around, talking and laughing. Foxy wasn't going to come out of the woods with all this activity.

And what had made her so sure Foxy would come back to the tent? Amber began to doubt that she had been in it at all last night. After the accident she had probably jumped from the car and taken off. She could be miles away by now.

Or she could have been badly hurt and crawled back into the swamp to die. Just because they hadn't found her body didn't mean she was lurking around here, waiting to be caught by Amber.

And if she did catch her, what was she going to tell her parents? If they knew who the dog really was, they would want to tell Jeff. They wouldn't understand that she had as much right to own Foxy as Jeff had.

Luckily they had never seen Foxy. Amber could say she was a stray. For all anybody knew, the people who dumped Foxy could have dumped more than one dog. That wasn't so unusual. If the Woodwards came back, they didn't have to see Foxy. Amber could keep her in the house until she was sure they had gone north again.

Her father had told Jeff that Foxy was dead. Amber was glad she'd kept the collar from the dead dog. If Jeff ever saw it, he would know right away it wasn't Foxy that her father had buried.

For a minute she saw Jeff's face as he lay on the stretcher last night, asking about Foxy, but she pushed the image away. He hadn't known Foxy very long. How bad could he feel?

It was getting harder and harder to stay still. Amber's sore muscles caused her to stand in an unnatural position that made her hurt even more. She tried to concentrate on thinking up a new name for Foxy, but she couldn't come up with anything that she liked.

Suddenly she saw animal eyes shining under the mangroves. She froze, waiting for whatever it was to approach the food she had put in front of the tent.

A raccoon. She might have known. Another raccoon joined the first one. They would eat everything before Foxy came, but she was afraid to chase them away. Foxy might be watching.

The raccoons tensed and stared into the darkness

behind the tent. Something must be back there. Another raccoon, Amber thought, but she held her breath and hoped.

The animal that trotted out of the shadows wasn't a raccoon. It was Foxy. She didn't seem to be hurt at all. Her head was up, her eyes bright, her ears swiveling back and forth. She expects to see Jeff, Amber thought.

Foxy chased the raccoons and ate the food they had left, then drank noisily from the bucket of water Amber had put out. She stuck her head in the tent, backed out again, and sniffed all along the edge. Nose to the ground, she ran under the picnic table and then headed for the trailer.

Oh, no, Amber thought, but Foxy didn't come behind the trailer. She just sniffed at the steps and the bottom of the door before turning back to the tent.

Go in, go in, Amber urged silently. Foxy hesitated at the opening for a moment and then cautiously entered the tent.

Amber came out from behind the trailer and moved to the tent entrance as quickly as she could. She tried to be quiet, but Foxy must have heard her or seen her because in the few seconds it took Amber to reach the tent Foxy was tearing at the back of it with her claws, trying to rip her way out.

"Wait, Foxy." Amber knelt and crawled into the tent. If she could get hold of her, Foxy would give up.

"Don't be scared, Foxy," she said, reaching out her hand.

Her fingers touched the dog's thick, rough coat. She had her. Then in one wild leap Foxy flung herself across the tent and out the opening.

Her rush knocked Amber off balance. Screaming, "Foxy!" she scrambled up and out of the tent, but she knew she had missed her chance. Foxy had escaped.

Amber's eyes strained to catch a glimpse of movement beyond the tent, but it was too dark to see anything. She slumped down on the picnic bench, fighting back tears of disappointment. Why did Foxy act that way? She only wanted to help, and look how Foxy treated her.

She sat there for a long time, feeling her resentment grow. Foxy was just a dog. She didn't hurt her feelings purposely. But she hurt them just the same. Well, she wouldn't put out any more food for her. It would serve Foxy right if she starved to death.

There was a rustling sound behind the tent, and Amber looked up in time to see something slink back into the shadows. An animal. And though she hadn't gotten a good look, she had seen enough to believe that it was Foxy. So she hadn't run away. She was just waiting until the coast was clear so that she could go back into the tent.

It must be more than just food that was drawing Foxy back. Amber wondered if she was remembering Jeff, feeling safer when she was where Jeff had been. Why couldn't she understand that she would be safe with Amber?

To think that Foxy was right there and Amber couldn't get her. She just wasn't quick enough. It would take another animal to catch Foxy.

Another animal. Why hadn't she thought of that before? Maybe she couldn't catch Foxy herself. But King could.

Chapter 17

Amber sat in front of the TV, trying to keep awake. She didn't see how she could be nervous and sleepy at the same time, but she was. She was trying to allow enough time for her parents to fall asleep before she left the house, but how much time was that?

Her head dropped forward, jerking her awake. This was stupid. She would have to leave now, or she might miss her chance altogether. If she made any noise, maybe her parents would think it was the TV.

It would be so much easier if she could tell them what she was doing, but she knew they wouldn't let her use King to catch Foxy if they knew. But this was the only way to get her. Maybe someday she would tell her father how she had done it, but she couldn't risk letting him know beforehand.

She unlocked the back door and fixed it so it wouldn't lock behind her. As soon as she stepped outside, King was up and growling. His chain rattled noisily. Amber ran to him and rubbed his head and ears, trying to calm him down.

"Be quiet, King. We're going for a walk," she whispered.

She picked up a length of rope she had put there earlier. When she caught Foxy, she would have to tie her up somewhere for the night and pretend to find her tomorrow. For now she tied it to King's collar and then unhooked his chain.

Right away he knew that he was free. It took all of Amber's strength to hold onto him. He pulled her this way and that, sniffing and examining everything they passed. At least he wasn't barking.

Amber hadn't realized that he was so wild. She had taken him for walks when he was a puppy, but for a long time now he had lived his life chained to a stake. Poor dog. Why had she neglected him like that?

He was really happy to be loose at last. Too happy. Amber had to keep jerking at the rope with both hands to force him in the direction she wanted to go.

For the first time she began to have doubts about her plan. She was quickly losing confidence in her ability to control King. Her mental picture of King cornering Foxy so she could grab her was completely unrealistic. She could see that now.

They had reached the edge of the Woodward campsite when Amber knew she wasn't going to try it. It was just too risky. She would have to think of some other way to catch Foxy.

She turned and tried to pull King along with her, but he was looking toward the tent, a low growl rumbling deep in his throat. Amber began to be afraid.

"Come on, King," she said, tugging on the rope.

At the sound of her voice a shadow moved at the tent entrance. King saw it, too. He leaped, and the rope burned Amber's palms as it whipped out of her grasp.

Foxy saw King coming. She darted from the tent a second too late. As Amber watched in horror, King hurled himself on top of her.

Foxy rolled over and away from him, leaped to her feet, and raced across the field with King only inches behind her. Amber stood frozen, her hands over her mouth. Foxy was heading for the woods. In its tangle of vines and thorns she might have a chance to escape. For a moment it seemed that she would make it. Then King lunged, knocking her to the ground.

"King, no!" Amber tried to yell, but her voice sounded breathless and weak. She ran across the field to the wildly thrashing dogs, but when she reached them, she was afraid. They were snarling like wolves. If she tried to separate them, would they turn on her?

She hesitated, breathing hard, until a yelp that was almost a shriek came from Foxy. Amber's heart seemed to stop. King was killing Foxy while she stood and watched. She had to do something.

She grabbed the rope she had tied to King's collar and yanked it hard, but he paid no attention. She kicked him, knocking him off balance; but he went right back at Foxy without a backward glance, and Amber saw with a sinking heart that Foxy wasn't fighting anymore.

In desperation she grabbed King's collar with both hands and twisted it hard, pulling it against his throat. He choked and tried to pull away, but Amber held on, throwing her whole body into the effort. She felt at that moment that she could kill King.

She wrestled with him, trying to keep the collar tight around his neck, but without the element of surprise she wasn't able to choke him again. At least she had gotten him away from Foxy.

King pawed at Amber and tried to shake her off, but she could see that he was enjoying the struggle. He thought it was a game. Amber could hardly believe it. How could he go from killing to playing just like that? Or were they the same thing to King? She maneuvered him toward the woods, away from Foxy, and while he leaped and frisked beside her, she grabbed the rope dangling from his collar and tied it around a tree.

She didn't wait to see if he would try to escape. With her heart in her throat, she ran to Foxy.

Chapter 18

Foxy was lying on her side with her head thrown back as if she had been gasping for breath. She was hardly breathing at all now. Her eyes were open, but she didn't seem to see. Her mouth was open, too, and her tongue was hanging out on the ground. Looking at her, Amber sank to her knees and began to cry.

"Oh, Foxy, I'm so sorry," she said sobbing.

A heaving breath jerked the dog's body, terrifying Amber.

"Don't die! Please don't die!" she begged.

She looked around frantically. She couldn't just sit here and watch Foxy bleed to death. What could she do?

She thought of the veterinarian across the highway. Dr. Gregg could help, but would he in the middle of the night like this?

There wasn't time to think about it. Foxy wouldn't last until morning. She needed treatment now.

Amber carefully gathered Foxy in her arms and stood up. The dog's head dropped back, her tongue lolling out of her mouth. Her fur was wet with blood and with King's saliva.

Amber began to run. She cut across the field, stumbling over the rough ground, reckless with haste. Foxy's head bobbed limply with each step.

The going was easier on the campground road, but the way seemed endless. *Hurry, hurry,* Amber's mind kept repeating, but she felt as if she were moving in slow motion.

There was no traffic on the highway. She darted across it and up the shell-bordered path to Dr. Gregg's front door. Still holding Foxy in her arms, she pushed the doorbell with her elbow.

She waited, wanting to scream with impatience and tension. Nothing happened. She rang the bell again. Why didn't someone answer? She felt Foxy's blood running down her arms, and fear shot through her. Even if help came, it might be too late. She laid the dog down on the step and began beating on the door with both fists.

A light went on in the house. At last. Someone was coming. She would have help.

Along with relief came a new worry. Dr. Gregg knew her. He would want to know what she was doing out at this time of night with an injured dog. What could she tell him?

She didn't want anyone to know the truth. It made

her sound so foolish. And he would tell her parents. Then she would have to admit what she had done and hear about it for the rest of her life.

The outside light went on, and Amber knew she couldn't be standing there when the door opened. She had to hide.

Leaving Foxy on the step, she ran around the corner of the house and kept running, heading for the dark mangrove swamp beyond the gravelly backyard. She crashed through the undergrowth until she tripped over a tangle of roots, and then she stayed where she'd fallen, pulling herself up into a crouch, trying to quiet her noisy breathing.

She waited there for a long time, terrified that someone would come looking for her or that the dogs in the kennels on the other side of the house would get her scent and begin to bark. But everything stayed quiet, and as her fear began to ebb, she realized how tired she was, sickeningly tired. Would she ever be back home, safe in her own bed? She wanted to crawl out of the mangroves and run back across the highway, but the effort seemed too much.

Then she had a thought that drove her to her feet and out of her hiding place. What if Dr. Gregg hadn't taken Foxy in? What if he had left her lying on the step to bleed to death?

She dashed across the yard and flattened herself against the wall of the house. Cautiously she worked her way to the front corner and then stood there, afraid to look.

The longer she hesitated, the surer she was that no one had answered her knock. Or someone had looked out, seen nobody, and gone back to bed. Oh, why had she run? How could she have left Foxy alone?

She forced herself to step around the side of the house and out into the open. The outside light was still on, but she was past caring if she was seen.

She looked at the step, and a surge of relief left her dizzy. Except for a dark stain where Foxy had lain, the step was empty. Foxy was being taken care of. She would be all right, Amber told herself firmly, but as she jogged back across the highway toward home, she thought, *What did I dump her like that for? Now how am I going to get her back?*

Chapter 19

After Amber had dragged King home and chained him up again, sneaked into the house, and crawled into bed, she could hardly believe she had gotten away with it. As far as she knew, no one had seen her. Her parents hadn't heard her. How had she done it?

She would make a good spy. No, she wouldn't. She never wanted to go through anything like that again. If you knew ahead of time that everything was going to work out, that was one thing. But she couldn't take the uncertainty.

She lay on her back, staring up at the ceiling, exhausted but too keyed up to sleep. She kept thinking about Foxy. What was happening to her right now? Dr. Gregg must be stitching her up, maybe even giving her a transfusion.

She wondered how long Foxy would have to stay at the vet's. How long would Dr. Gregg keep an ownerless dog around? She frowned worriedly into the darkness. He might give Foxy to someone else. Her heart thumped. He might take her to the pound.

She tossed restlessly on the bed. Why had she taken Foxy there anyway? She should have done something herself or at least tried. What had made her so sure Dr. Gregg would help her? After all, why should he? A horrible thought tied her stomach into a knot. He wouldn't put her to sleep, would he?

She pulled the pillow over her head and tried not to think. There wasn't anything she could do now. Either Dr. Gregg would treat Foxy or he wouldn't. Either Foxy would live or she would die.

That rotten King. What happened tonight was all his fault. If Foxy died, she would get rid of him. She would take him to the SPCA, and she didn't care what they did with him. He was a vicious, mean dog.

It was nearly morning. She had to get some sleep. But another nagging thought began to torment her. She told herself not to be silly, but the idea wouldn't go away. How did she know that Foxy was really with Dr. Gregg? What if, while she was hiding in the mangroves, Foxy had dragged herself off the step and away from the house? What if Dr. Gregg had never seen her at all?

Amber rolled over and shut her eyes determinedly. She wasn't going to worry about it. It was impossible. Foxy had been almost unconscious from shock and loss of blood. She wasn't able to stand, much less walk.

But she was a tough little dog, even though she was afraid of everything. If there were any way she could have crawled away from the house, she would have done it.

Amber saw she wasn't going to be able to sleep. It was getting light anyway. She rolled out of bed and looked under it to make sure her clothes from last night were well out of sight. They were too dirty and bloodstained to put in the hamper. Her mother would ask questions she wouldn't want to answer. She would have to do something with them sometime, but not now.

She stayed in the shower for a long time, just standing there with her eyes shut. It felt good, but she couldn't stay there all day, much as she felt like it. Drying off, she noticed long scratches on her arms and legs. When had they happened? When she was fighting with King probably or when she'd run through the swamp. She hadn't felt anything at the time.

Her mind started on Foxy again. Was she all right or not? Was she at Dr. Gregg's being cared for, or was she gone?

The only way to be sure was to run over there and see. But how could she do that without giving herself away? What could she say? "Hi, did anybody leave a dog on your doorstep lately?" Or, "Hello, Dr. Gregg, did an injured dog ring your doorbell last night?" No, there was no way to do it. It was too soon to go over there asking questions. It would be too suspicious.

The smell of coffee drew Amber to the kitchen. Her parents looked surprised to see her.

"What are you doing up?" her mother asked. "You don't have to go to school, remember?"

"You look bad," her father said, setting a place for her.

"Do you wonder, after what she's been through?" her mother asked.

Amber's stomach tightened. *How does she know?* she thought in a panic before she realized that her mother was referring to the car accident. The accident. Amber had almost forgotten it.

"I'm going to see the Woodwards later today," her father said. "Think you might want to come?"

Amber hesitated. "I'll let you know," she said finally.

In a way she would like to see Jeff, but she would feel a little funny talking to him. Not that she felt guilty. She hadn't done anything to feel guilty about. But she wouldn't want to talk to Jeff about Foxy. She remembered how he had looked in the ambulance when he asked about her. She'd rather not see that expression again.

Amber poured some juice, buttered a muffin. She thought she was hungry, but with the first bite her appetite left her. She sat staring at her plate, fighting a sudden desire to cry. She looked up and saw her parents watching her anxiously.

"Maybe you'd like an egg," her mother said.

Amber shook her head. She wanted to tell her that

she was all right, but her throat felt blocked.

"I think you're having a delayed reaction to the accident," her father said. "Why don't you go back to bed for a while? I'll check with you when I'm ready to go to the hospital."

"Okay." Amber tried to smile at them as she left the kitchen. She went to her bedroom and stood in the doorway, thinking. She couldn't go back to bed. She would just continue to toss and turn and worry. What she had to do was get to Dr. Gregg's. Until she knew for sure that Foxy was safe, she would be a nervous wreck.

What excuse could she give Dr. Gregg for wanting to see all the dogs in his kennel? She couldn't think of anything that seemed reasonable. And if he questioned her, she knew she would get all mixed up and guilty-acting.

If she could wait a few days, it would be better, but she was afraid to wait.

Well, standing here wasn't doing any good. Maybe some exercise would stir up her brain. She went outside and watched coldly as King strained toward her, wagging his tail. She didn't think she could ever like him again.

He had a gash across his nose that was caked with dried blood. Poor Foxy. She had tried.

Amber turned her back on King and headed toward the Woodward campsite. She told herself it was a waste of time, but she wanted to look in Jeff's tent. Even if

Foxy had crawled away from the vet's, she couldn't have gotten this far, Amber was sure. But she had to check.

She tried not to let herself hope, but her breathing quickened as she knelt and peered through the opening of the tent.

It was empty, of course. She had known it would be empty, hadn't she? She crawled inside and picked up the stained pillow that had first made her suspect that Foxy was nearby. It was dry now. She turned it over and lay down with her cheek against it. Why did she feel so bad? She had known Foxy wouldn't be here.

Chapter 20

Amber woke up soaked with perspiration. The tent was like an oven. She dragged herself out and stood up, feeling groggy and sick. How long had she been sleeping? Hours, it felt like. She hadn't meant to fall asleep.

The air revived her, cooling her skin and clearing her head. She was starving suddenly. She headed for home, fluffing out her damp hair with her fingers as she went.

She was finishing her second peanut butter sandwich when her father came into the kitchen.

"Feeling better?" he asked.

Amber nodded. "Did you go to the hospital?"

"Just got back." He dropped the car keys onto the counter and sat down across the table from her. "I looked for you."

"I went for a walk," Amber said.

"Well, I saw the Woodwards. They're doing well, considering. They asked about you."

"Did they?" Amber felt that she should say more, but she didn't know what. "How's Jeff?" she asked.

"About the same. I took him the collar."

Amber stiffened. "What collar?"

"Foxy's. I saw it on your bureau when I was looking for you."

Amber felt as if she'd been punched in the stomach. "What did Jeff say?" She was afraid of the answer, but she had to ask.

"He was asleep. I left it with his father."

"What did *he* say?"

"He said he'd give it to Jeff when he woke up."

Amber was exasperated. Her father wasn't telling her anything. She couldn't come right out and ask what she wanted to know. Did Jeff's father realize that the collar wasn't Foxy's? If so, did he understand what that meant?

There was no use asking any more questions. If Mr. Woodward had noticed anything, he hadn't told her father.

She stood up. "I guess I'll go out again," she said.

Her father stood up, too. "I know you wanted to wait," he said, "but I thought Jeff should have the collar."

"I know. It's okay," Amber said. She left the kitchen and ran outside.

Now what? Jeff knew, or he would realize soon, that Foxy could be alive. What would he do? This was going to complicate things.

Well, she couldn't afford to stand around worrying

about it. She had wasted enough time. She had to find out if Foxy was at Dr. Gregg's and, if so, how hard it was going to be to get her back.

The highway was busy. Amber waited for a break in the traffic and ran across. She followed the shell-bordered path to the doorstep where she had left Foxy last night, keeping her eyes away from the bloodstains she knew must still be there.

She opened the door. The waiting room seemed crowded with dogs and cats and humans, who turned and stared at her as she stood there. Without entering, she closed the door.

This wasn't going to work. She couldn't just walk in and start asking questions. She needed an animal, some excuse for visiting a vet. But the only animal she had was King, and he would tear the place apart.

A dog in the waiting room yapped, setting off an explosion of barks from the kennel. The kennel! That was the place to check first anyway.

Amber hurried toward the long, low building, hoping for a chance to look around before anyone noticed her. There was a screened door at the front, and she peered through it into a small office. It was empty. So far, so good. She opened the door quietly and slipped inside.

A big gray cat was crouched on the floor beside a pet carrier. It stood up and meowed, but Amber barely glanced at it. She walked straight to the cages she could see in a room beyond the office.

The first cage held a cat. The rest would, too, then, but she checked them all just in case. All cats.

"Can I help you?"

Amber jumped guiltily. A teenage girl was standing in the doorway.

"I was just looking at the cats," Amber said.

"Is yours here?" the girl asked.

"No. I just like animals." It sounded like a feeble reason to Amber, but the girl seemed to accept it. She was probably an animal lover herself to be working here, Amber thought, so she asked, "Can I look at the dogs?"

"Sure." The girl led Amber through another door to the dog kennel, two rows of wire enclosures with a cement walk between them. "Go ahead," she said. "I have a cage to clean."

Amber tried to make herself walk slowly down the line of pens, but she couldn't do it. Heart pounding, she glanced from one cage to the other, expecting in each one to see Foxy's timid brown eyes gazing up at her.

The dogs were excited at seeing a stranger. Some of them barked furiously at Amber. Others pushed their noses against the wire and wagged their tails. Amber ignored them. The only dog she was interested in was Foxy.

Be here, Foxy, be here, she begged silently, but it didn't take long to see that she wasn't. Disappointment choked Amber. A little dog in the last cage yipped at her, and she knelt down and scratched its fuzzy head through the wire while she tried to control her feelings.

Don't give up, she told herself. *Not yet.*

She gave the little dog a last scratch and stood up. She wanted to ask the kennel girl some questions, but she wasn't sure how to put them.

"Do you ever give dogs away?" she finally asked. It sounded as if she were asking for a free dog, but she couldn't help it. She needed to find out what they had done with Foxy.

"Oh, no. They all belong to somebody." The girl put a bowl of water on the floor of the cage she was cleaning. "Most are boarding because their owners are away. Some are recovering from surgery."

"Oh." The girl was just telling her things she already knew. She tried again. "What do you do with dogs the owners don't come back for?"

"That's never happened," the girl said. "It's funny you should say that, though."

"Why?" Amber tried to look only mildly interested, but it wasn't easy. She knew the girl was going to tell her about Foxy.

"Somebody dropped a dog off here last night."

"You mean, just left it here?" Amber hoped she sounded surprised.

"Just left it. It had been in a fight. Dr. Gregg was furious." The girl laughed.

"What did he do?" Amber asked, trying to laugh, too.

"He stitched her up, but he's still furious."

Amber took a deep breath. "Is the dog all right?"

"I think she will be. Want to see her?"

Amber smiled. "Sure."

"I've been fixing up this cage for her. I'll get her."

The girl walked toward the office and stopped suddenly in the doorway. "Uh-oh," she said.

"What is it?" Amber pushed past the girl and saw what she was looking at. The bottom of the screened door had been ripped through.

The gray cat was peering into the pet carrier. The girl pushed it out of the way and looked inside.

"She's gone," she said. "Dr. Gregg will have a fit."

Amber ran to the door and looked out. There was no sign of Foxy.

She turned to the girl, who still stood there, looking stunned.

"Come on. Let's look for her," she said.

"She seemed so weak," the girl said. "I never thought she would do anything like this."

"Come on," Amber urged. "She can't be far away."

"At least this dog didn't belong to anybody," the girl said, following Amber outside. "It's not like I've lost somebody's pet."

Amber wasn't paying attention. "She probably headed for the swamp," she said. "You try that part, and I'll look over here."

"What makes you so sure she didn't run to the house or across the road?"

Amber couldn't tell her that Foxy wouldn't do either

of those things. She was afraid of cars. She was even more afraid of people. She had to be in the swamp.

"We're wasting time," she said, ignoring the question.

"The dog we're looking for is small and black with a long, fluffy tail," the girl said. "Or do I have to tell you that?"

Amber looked at her and turned away without answering. So she knew. Had she suspected all along? Well, it didn't matter now. Finding Foxy was all that mattered.

The girl was walking along the edge of the swamp, whistling. That was wasted effort, Amber knew. Foxy wouldn't come to either of them willingly.

But she was probably too weak to go far. There was a good chance she was holed up somewhere close by. Amber chose a place where the footing seemed fairly good and plunged into the mangrove swamp.

After a few minutes of searching she lost her optimism. How could you find anything in here? There were leaves and logs and countless tangles of roots covering what ground there was. There was water, too, and soon Amber's sneakers squelched with every step. Before she was out of sight of the kennel, she saw the girl go back to it. She hadn't looked long. She probably thought the dog would come back when it was hungry, like any normal dog. She didn't know that Foxy wasn't a normal dog.

The longer Amber searched, the more useless it

seemed. How could you find one little dog in this huge swamp, especially a dog that didn't want to be found?

Climbing over roots and squishing through mucky water tired Amber out. She found a log that was high enough out of the water to be fairly dry and sat down on it.

It made her sick to remember how close she had been to Foxy without knowing it. If only she had stopped to look in the pet carrier. She could have picked it up and carried Foxy home before anyone noticed. She had thought she was being such a detective, asking questions to make the girl tell her about Foxy. And she had walked right past the dog.

She got up and began slogging through the mangroves again, but she was becoming more and more sure that she wouldn't find Foxy. She had botched her last chance.

It suddenly hit her that it had been Foxy's last chance, too. She had been in bad shape when Jeff found her. She was in worse shape now, weak from loss of blood, maybe confused from drugs.

She would probably be too sick to look for food tonight. There was no food here. She would have to cross the road and get to the campground. Amber remembered how afraid Foxy had been of cars in Key West. She didn't believe she would have the nerve to cross the highway.

"Oh, Foxy, please come," she called, but she knew it

was hopeless. Foxy would never come to her, no matter how scared she was or how lonely or sick.

Foxy loved Jeff. She trusted him. Ever since the accident she had been looking for him. And now that Foxy was too weak to search, Amber knew that she would stay wherever she was hiding and wait for Jeff until she died.

Chapter 21

Foxy lay in a pile of dead, wet leaves, panting heavily. She heard the crunch of footsteps and the snap of branches. She knew Amber was searching for her, and she was afraid.

When the footsteps seemed close, Foxy's eyes rolled toward the sound, but she made no move to hide or escape. She had used the last of her strength to flee the kennel.

An adult key deer, no bigger than a colt, slipped noiselessly through the brush. It glanced at Foxy without interest, intent on the greater danger behind it, and vanished into the undergrowth.

Amber called out once, and then for a long while there was silence. Foxy's panting gradually stopped, and she lay still, except when shudders convulsed her. After a while she forgot that she was afraid and sick, forgot that she was hiding. Her open eyes glazed over, and her body settled deeper into the bed of leaves.

Chapter 22

Jeff walked down the hall to his father's room, feeling silly in his borrowed robe and paper slippers.

He found his father watching TV from his bed with his eyes half-closed.

"Soap operas will rot your mind," Jeff said.

His father opened his eyes and sat up. "That's what I thought yesterday," he said. "Today I can't wait to see what happens tomorrow."

They both laughed.

"How's your knee?" Jeff asked.

"I can't tell. I'm still not supposed to put any weight on it. Tomorrow I'm demanding a wheelchair."

"I thought I'd go down and see Mom," Jeff said.

"Do you feel up to it?"

"Sure. I did yesterday, but they wouldn't let me go."

"Your mother was pretty much out of it yesterday

anyway. At least that's how she sounded on the phone."

"I know," Jeff said. "I'll stop by on my way back and let you know how she looks."

"Good. Oh, wait a minute." His father took a paper bag from his nightstand and handed it to Jeff. "Amber's father was here while you were sleeping. He brought you a present."

Jeff opened the bag and held up the brown leather collar he found inside. "What's this?"

An odd expression came over his father's face. "I wish I'd looked before I gave it to you," he said.

Jeff examined the collar. His father seemed to expect him to recognize it, but he was sure he had never seen it before.

"I didn't want to tell you until you felt better," his father was saying. "I'm sorry, Jeff."

Jeff watched his father's face. Something bad was coming. He braced himself and waited.

"It's about Foxy."

"What about her?" Jeff asked quickly.

His father sighed unhappily. "Jeff, Foxy died in the crash."

Jeff stood very still. Maybe if he didn't move, he could hold back his feelings.

How could Foxy be dead? He had been thinking about her ever since the accident, wondering if she was eating, hoping she didn't miss him too much. And all the time she was dead.

"I want to see her," he said through stiff lips.

"Amber's father buried her. She was killed instantly, he said. She didn't suffer."

"Have you known all along?"

"Just since yesterday. I couldn't tell you. If I'd known what was in that bag, I wouldn't have given it to you."

Jeff glanced at the collar he was holding. "You mean this?"

His father nodded. "I guess he thought you should have it."

What for? Jeff wondered, and then it came to him. "He thinks it's Foxy's collar," he said. "So do you, don't you?"

"He took it off her before he buried her," his father said gently.

"Then he didn't bury Foxy." Relief made Jeff laugh out loud. His father looked at him in astonishment, and that made him laugh again. "Don't you remember Mom buying her that string collar? With beads? It wasn't anything like this."

He could see that his father did remember, even though he was shaking his head. "That's impossible. He couldn't make such a mistake."

"He never saw Foxy," Jeff reminded him.

"But Amber did. She wouldn't let him bury a strange dog."

"You don't know Amber." Jeff stood there thinking. All this time he had thought Foxy was at Amber's. Instead she was alone, running wild again. His throat tightened. She might be hurt. She might be looking for him.

He put the collar back in the bag and handed it to his father. "Dad, I need some money."

"Money?"

"Taxi money. I have to get to the campground."

"Now, wait," his father said. "You're in no condition to go anywhere."

"Yes, I am. Dad, please." He hated the way his voice broke.

"You can't leave the hospital," his father said firmly. "Not yet. Look, call Amber—"

"There's no use calling Amber."

"Call her father. Tell him what you think. Ask him to look for Foxy." He touched Jeff's arm sympathetically. "You couldn't do any more than that if you were there yourself."

That was probably true, Jeff thought, but still, he wanted to be there. He had to be there.

Restlessness seized him. He couldn't stand still any longer.

"I'll go see Mom now," he said. "Then I'll call Amber's father."

There must be more that he could do, but what? He couldn't think. In a few minutes he had gone from believing Foxy was fine, to hearing she was dead, to finding out nobody really knew where or how she was.

If she was alive, she was looking for him—if she

wasn't too hurt or too weak. He had to get to her. As soon as he was released, he would go to the campground and look for her. But when would that be? How long could Foxy wait?

Chapter 23

Jeff's mother was waiting for him. He was shocked at how she looked, but he pretended not to notice. She didn't pretend, though.

"Jeff, your face," she said, and he was afraid she was going to cry.

"It doesn't hurt." He pulled a chair close to her bed and sat down.

His mother reached out and ran her finger down the cut on his cheek. "That's going to leave a scar," she said regretfully.

"I don't mind a scar," Jeff said. "But I hope the bruises clear up. I don't want to go through life with a blue and purple face."

"How about green and yellow? That's what you'll be by tomorrow." She grinned at him, and then her face fell again. "Oh, Jeff, isn't this awful?"

He had been going to tell her about Foxy. He had

hoped she might side with him and let him go to look for her, but now he dropped the idea. She was worried enough.

"Don't feel bad," he said. "We're all going to be okay."

She nodded, but she was still holding back tears.

"This just gives us a longer vacation," he said.

"Look at you trying to cheer me up." His mother reached for his hand and held it in both of hers. "I wanted you to have good memories of the keys," she said. "I was so happy here before."

"In your 'before Jeff' days, you mean."

His mother smiled dreamily, and something twisted in Jeff's chest.

"Then I came along and spoiled everything," he said bitterly.

His mother looked at him in surprise. "You didn't spoil anything." Then she laughed. "But you really changed things."

"I know. You left the keys just because of me."

"We would have gone back anyway."

"But not for a long time," Jeff said. "I stopped all your fun."

"Come here, Jeff," his mother said.

He sat on the bed, and she put a hand on each of his shoulders.

"You didn't spoil things. You put meaning in our lives," she said. "Don't you understand that?"

Jeff squirmed uncomfortably. Why had he started this? "No," he said.

"Well then, just believe it," his mother said. "You can understand later."

An aide came in, carrying a food tray. Jeff started to stand up, but his mother held him.

"Wait," she said. "I'm trying to find an unbruised place on your face to kiss."

"There isn't one," Jeff said, but she kissed him anyway.

"I'd better go back before somebody grabs my tray," he said.

"All right. Enjoy your dinner. And, Jeff—"

"What?"

"Try not to be so dumb."

The way she said it made him laugh. "Okay," he promised.

He took the elevator back up to his floor and stopped in to give his father a report. When he got back to his own room, the phone was ringing. He smiled as he answered, expecting to hear, "Have you stopped being dumb?" but it wasn't his mother on the line.

"Jeff, is that you?" a voice asked shrilly, and it took him a minute to realize it was Amber.

"I've been calling and calling." She was crying so hard he could hardly understand her. "Foxy's dying. You've got to come right away."

"What's happened?" Jeff felt as if he couldn't breathe.

"Foxy's hiding in the swamp. She'll die if you don't get her out. Oh, Jeff, hurry!"

"I can't leave here. They won't let me." He felt that any second he would be as hysterical as Amber.

"Then she'll die!" Amber wailed. "I've killed her!"

What did she mean? He made a determined effort to calm himself.

"Amber, be quiet a minute." He glanced around and lowered his voice. "Listen. I'll get out somehow, but I don't have a way to get to the campground. Can your father come after me?"

There was a silence on the other end of the line.

"Amber?"

"I don't want him to know," she said in a small voice.

"That you called me?"

"No, I don't want him to know what I did to Foxy." She started to cry noisily again. "She'll die if you don't come!"

"Then tell your father," Jeff said. "Meet me in the parking lot. I don't know how long it'll take me to get out, but wait."

"But, Jeff—"

He hung up. There was no use arguing on and on. He wasn't even sure this wasn't some crazy trick she was playing. But if she wanted him there as much as she said she did, she would ask her father to get him. She'd probably think up a big lie first to cover whatever it was she didn't want him to know, but she would get him there.

What did she mean about killing Foxy? He had to get to the campground to find out what was going on.

Even if her father didn't come, even if this was one of her mean practical jokes, he had to go. He couldn't spend this whole night wondering about Foxy without doing anything.

How hard was it to walk out of a hospital? Could they keep you if you wanted to leave? Even if they didn't stop him, they would tell his father. He would have to leave without anyone seeing him.

Clothes! Where were his clothes? Nothing was hanging in the closet. Were his things still in the emergency room? Or lost?

There was a large brown bag on the floor of the closet, and Jeff looked in it hopefully. Relief washed over him. Everything was there, even his torn and bloodstained windbreaker. Now he wouldn't have to try to leave in his robe.

How much time did he have? He didn't want to leave too soon. Someone might notice he was missing while he was still waiting in the parking lot.

His dinner was on a tray by his bed. Even though his stomach was one big knot, he forced himself to eat. He felt weak enough without letting hunger make him weaker.

After he had eaten, he stood in the doorway, looking out into the hall. How could you sneak anywhere in a hospital? There were so many people.

He decided to wait fifteen minutes and then dress quickly and head for the stairs. That seemed safer than waiting for an elevator. If people saw him, they might think he was going down to see his mother.

He wished he could tell his mother what was happening. He had a feeling she would let him go. She would be almost as worried about Foxy as he was. But that was just the reason he couldn't tell her.

His phone rang and he jumped. It was his father.

"Jeff, come on down the hall. I want to see you," he said, and he sounded mad.

Chapter 24

"What's going on?" Jeff's father demanded as soon as he saw him.

Jeff couldn't answer. He swallowed nervously, and his father went on impatiently. "Amber's father just called me. What have you and Amber been hatching up?"

Jeff knew then that Foxy was really in danger. Amber had asked her father to come for him. She wouldn't have taken a joke that far.

"Did he tell you about Foxy?" he asked.

"It doesn't matter about Foxy. I told him you couldn't leave here. He knew that anyway."

"But Foxy needs me," Jeff said. "I have to get her."

"No, you don't. You have to stay here and rest. Don't you realize what you've been through?"

Jeff tried to speak calmly and reasonably. "Foxy's afraid of everyone but me. She'll die if I don't get her."

"She's lived wild most of her life," his father said. "A few more nights won't make much difference."

"Yes, they will." Jeff felt his control slipping. "She was starving when we found her. Now she might be hurt. Dad, please, please, I have to find her!"

"Look at yourself," his father said. "You're shaking all over. You're probably in worse shape than Foxy."

"No, I'm not," Jeff said thickly.

His father watched him unhappily. "This leg!" he burst out suddenly. "I wish I could go. I'd give that dog good reason to be scared. I'd drag her out by the scruff of her neck!"

"Dad . . ." Jeff began, ready for one more try, but his father stopped him.

"I hate having to say no, but I'm more worried about you than about Foxy."

That was it then. There was nothing more to say.

"Sit down and watch TV with me awhile," his father said in a different tone.

"I don't feel like TV." Jeff turned to leave.

"Jeff," his father said, "don't bother your mother with this."

"I won't." It was just what he had been going to do.

He went back to his room and sat on the bed, staring at the wall. What now? He couldn't seem to think. Disappointment had drained all his energy.

He lay back on the bed and thought about Foxy, the way her dark eyes followed every move he made and the way she stayed as close to him as she could get.

Where was she right now? What was she feeling? She must be wondering where he was and why he didn't come back.

He remembered how wild she had seemed the first night he had seen her outside his tent, with her foxlike muzzle and pointed ears. But she hadn't been wild, only desperate.

He thought of the way she had seemed to cling to him the night of the storm. She had trusted him to protect her. Now she was alone again. Did she understand that he hadn't wanted to leave her?

The phone rang, and he answered it listlessly.

"Jeff, it's Amber." Her whisper was almost too soft to hear.

He sat up and held the receiver tightly against his ear.

"Can't you talk louder?" he asked.

"No, they'll hear. Listen, I've got a ride for you."

"To the campground?" Jeff was whispering, too.

"Yes," she hissed. "Be in the parking lot at midnight."

"I'll try," Jeff said, and he heard her hang up.

Again he had the uneasy feeling that Amber was up to something. If she was serious, why did she have to be so dramatic? All that whispering. And why midnight? Why not 11:30 or 1:00 A.M.? The last time he talked to her she was crying her head off, and now she was playing secret agent.

There were questions he had wanted to ask. For one

thing, where exactly was he supposed to look for Foxy? There were a lot of mangroves.

And whom should he look for in the parking lot? She could at least have told him what kind of car to expect.

Well, if there were any way for him to get to the parking lot at midnight, he would be there. He would leave the details up to Amber. He didn't really have any choice.

For now there was a whole long evening to get through. Part of it would be taken up visiting each of his parents. That was going to be hard. He wouldn't feel right with them, knowing what he was planning. He had never purposely gone against something they felt strongly about. It wasn't a good feeling. But it seemed to him that it was a question of life or death.

He started to consider what he would do with Foxy if he found her and decided not to worry about it until the time came. Another thing to put out of his mind was what his father might do if he found out about this.

He should try to sleep a little if he could. His father was right about how shaky he was. He hadn't known it took so long to get over being knocked out.

He could feel himself getting nervous. He took some deep breaths to calm himself, but they didn't help much. It was going to be a long night.

Chapter 25

Jeff woke with a jolt. He jumped out of bed and then had to hold onto the table until a wave of black dizziness passed. What time was it? He was almost afraid to look, and when he did step to the doorway and check the hall clock, his fears were confirmed. Twelve-thirty! How could he have done that? He had thought he was too excited to sleep soundly.

He dressed as fast as he could, clumsy with haste, sending mental messages to the car he was supposed to meet at midnight: *Wait. I'll be there. Wait.*

He put the robe over his clothes and then stood still, overcome with something like stage fright. He couldn't make himself move. How could he ever hope to get out of here? Someone was bound to see him. Someone would stop him and tell his father. He would get in all kinds of trouble.

But nobody else could help Foxy.

He decided that as soon as the hall was clear, he

would head for the stairs. Once he started, he would have to keep going. If anyone saw him or called to him, he would run.

He took a deep breath and walked to the door. The hallway was empty. He walked quickly to the stairwell, a few doors down from his room. As he did, a nurse came out of a room at the other end of the hall. He ducked through the door and ran down the stairs as fast as he could. Had she seen him? Fear that she had made him go even faster.

On the main floor he threw the robe into a corner and opened the door slowly. Peering around it, he saw that he would never be able to walk out the front door the way he had hoped to. To reach it, he would have to pass the admitting desk, and there were several people working there.

Across the hall the elevator bell pinged. The nurse from upstairs! Was she coming after him? He turned back to the stairs and ran down another flight.

Now where was he? It looked like a storeroom. He could hear voices nearby, but he couldn't see anyone.

There was a door at the far end of the room. It led outside; Jeff was sure of it. But was it locked? He would have to step out in the open to find out. He wasn't sure where the men that he heard were, but he couldn't wait around.

He made a dash for the door and turned the knob. In another second he was standing on a loading platform in the dark, breezy night.

"Hey," someone yelled just before the door slammed behind him.

Jeff jumped from the platform. Stars exploded in his head as he landed, but he couldn't let the pain stop him. He had to hide.

He sprinted across a driveway and down an embankment into a mangrove tangle. He pushed deeper into the mangroves until suddenly he was out of them again, and he realized he was standing up to his knees in water. He had walked right out into the ocean. There were no waves here. The surf broke miles out against the reef. But it was the same ocean, full of all the things he had seen in the aquarium. He hoped the sharks were busy somewhere else.

He stood in the water listening. He heard the door slam once and then again. Had someone come out and gone back in again? Or had two people come out? Were they looking for him? Or waiting for him to show himself? Finally he knew he couldn't stand there any longer. It was a warm night, but not warm enough for this.

He waded back through the mangroves until he could see the hospital and loading platform. There was no one around as far as he could tell.

Should he make a run for the parking lot? He stood there, irresolute, hearing the rattle of palm fronds in the sea breeze and the water gently lapping the coral shore. It was quiet and lonely, but instead of being afraid, he felt a part of the wildness. For a moment he had a feeling of what the keys must have been before civilization set out to tame them, and he felt sorry.

There was still no sign of anyone. It must be one o'clock by now. He would have to chance it. He broke out of the mangroves on a run and raced for the parking lot. Nobody yelled at him. Nobody followed.

He hid behind a van and tried to catch his breath. He was in a cold sweat, and for a minute he thought he was going to be sick; but he fought down the feeling and scanned the lot. There were plenty of cars, but none seemed to be occupied. He stepped out where he could be seen. He didn't know whom to look for, but whoever was coming after him did.

Nobody approached him. Could they have gone? Would they have given up on him already? They should have known that he might not be able to get out exactly at midnight.

Well, he was out now. What should he do? He couldn't just go back inside and forget it. If Foxy had needed him so badly before, she must still need him. He would just have to walk to the campground.

He started off briskly, trying to act as if it weren't unusual for him to be out walking at one in the morning. Then he wondered why he was feeling so guilty. It wasn't illegal to be out at night, was it?

Of course, if the hospital people realized that he had walked out, they would probably look for him. Maybe even call the police. He looked around and began to walk faster. If he saw a patrol car, he would hide.

But he hadn't walked far before he came to the first

of a series of bridges he would have to cross before he reached the campground. There was nowhere to hide on the bridge, and it was a long one. A lot longer than he remembered.

Here goes nothing, he thought. He started across the bridge, running at first, but the jolting hurt his head. He slowed down to a walk, but soon even that hurt, each footstep bringing a sickening pain.

He tried not to think about how he felt. Foxy probably felt worse. No, he couldn't think about her either.

He looked out over the bridge at the miles and miles of water, on one side Florida Bay, on the other the Atlantic Ocean. He thought of all the little keys out there, the ones the highway hadn't touched, crowded with sleeping pelicans and cormorants and herons, waiting for morning to start their day of fishing. But the fish were getting harder and harder to find. That meant every year there would be fewer pelicans and cormorants and herons. Suddenly it seemed terrible to him.

He thought of the agent the plume hunters had killed. He must have felt like this. Had he known the danger he was in? *I'll look the story up in the library,* Jeff told himself. *That is, if I get through tonight.*

The bridge went on forever. How could he have thought he could walk to the campground? He couldn't even get to the next key. He was light-headed with exhaustion, but he trudged on because it was easier than deciding what else to do.

A car driving toward him caught his attention. It was

going very slowly, weaving slightly and straddling the center line. A truck going the other way blew its horn, and the car moved so far to the right that it scraped the curb. When the road was clear, it wavered back to the center again.

Drunk driver, Jeff thought. *Or some kids looking for trouble.* He walked faster and stared straight ahead, hoping to get by without being noticed.

With a screech of tires the car rocked to a stop beside him. His heart jumped into his throat, but he kept walking.

He heard a voice squeal, "Jeff, get in quick!" and he turned unbelievingly.

It was Amber. Driving. At least it looked like her, but it couldn't be. He must be sicker than he thought.

"Will you come on? We have to hurry!"

It wasn't a hallucination. That snippy voice could belong to only one person.

Jeff walked to the car. He was tired and confused, but he was very clear on one thing. He wasn't going to ride with anyone who drove like Amber.

"Move over," he ordered. He was a little surprised when she did. Maybe she didn't trust her driving either.

He slid behind the wheel and tried to pretend he knew what he was doing. The only times he had driven a car were in the school parking lot with his father beside him, but Amber didn't need to know that.

He gave the car too much gas, then overreacted and

jammed on the brakes. He glanced at Amber, expecting a remark, but she just said, "Your face is a mess."

"Thanks." He drove to the end of the bridge and pulled into a gas station to turn around. The distance he had so painfully walked didn't take any time in a car.

"Why didn't you wait for me?" Amber asked.

"You said twelve," he reminded her.

"My parents went to bed late. You should have waited," she complained. "What if I'd missed you?"

"Since there's only one road down the keys, it wasn't likely."

Amber fidgeted beside him, turning to look out the back, leaning over to check the speedometer.

"Can't you drive faster?" she asked.

"I don't want to have an accident in a stolen car," Jeff said irritably. What a pain she was.

Amber looked interested. "Is it stealing when it's your parents' car?"

"There must be some law against what you did. What we're both doing."

"Well, how else could we get Foxy?" Amber asked reasonably.

Jeff stopped himself from answering. Why was he letting himself be pulled into these dumb arguments? He needed all his concentration for driving.

He saw now that he could never have walked to the campground. Even if he had been unhurt, it would have taken hours. What had made him attempt it? He wondered if his judgment was impaired from the head injury. He knew that normally he would never act the way he had tonight. Maybe for the rest of his life he would do goofy things. Like Amber.

"Why were you so excited this afternoon, crying and all?" he asked.

Amber looked uncomfortable. "I didn't want Foxy to die."

"Your father seemed to think she was already dead."

Amber's face went blank. "Did he?" she asked, and Jeff knew things had happened that she would never tell him.

Did she really know where Foxy was? Or was this her idea of fun?

"What makes you so sure I'll find Foxy?" he asked.

"She's waiting for you," Amber said confidently. She seemed to think it was an answer. "After you get her," she went on eagerly, "I'll take care of her until you get out of the hospital."

Jeff shook his head. "I'm not going back to the hospital."

Amber looked stricken. "But you have to."

"I don't need the hospital. I can live in my tent until my parents are better."

"I wanted to take care of Foxy." Amber sounded so disappointed that he felt sorry for her in spite of himself.

"You can help me," he said. "If I find her."

"Big deal," she said sulkily, and he stopped being sorry for her.

He had expected to drive down the campground road, but Amber had him pull over just before they reached the turn.

"That's where Foxy is," she said, and Jeff looked where she pointed. It was like looking into a big black hole.

"I'll never find Foxy in there," he protested.

"She'll find you," Amber said.

Chapter 26

Jeff got out of the car and started across the lawn. He looked back once and saw Amber watching him solemnly through the window. She didn't look as confident as she claimed to be.

At the edge of the swamp he stopped. It was eerily quiet and pitch-black. He couldn't tell what was solid ground and what was water. As his eyes adjusted a little, he could see mangrove roots twisting away into the darkness like a million snakes. Some of those roots were probably real snakes. He didn't see how he could go in there.

But Amber said that was where Foxy was.

"Foxy!" he yelled. "It's me!"

The dogs in the kennel went wild. Jeff dived into the mangroves and crouched where he could see the house. He half expected lights to flash on and someone to run outside, waving a shotgun. Cold water seeping into his shoes brought him back to reality. The dogs probably carried on like that every time a raccoon strolled by. No one was likely to come out after him.

As the dogs gradually calmed down, Jeff realized that the swamp wasn't quiet at all. All around were stealthy little rustles and gurgles and plops. When he stood up, something dropped out of the branches near him and splashed away noisily. Jeff suppressed a yell and made himself stand still until his breathing returned to normal.

A few yards ahead of him a small form was huddled against a log. Had it been there all the time? He bent down and tried to force his eyes to see clearly, but it was just too dark.

"Is that you, Foxy?" he whispered. He approached the black shape cautiously, not sure whether it would run away or leap at his throat. He didn't know until he was close enough to touch it that he was stalking a mass of decaying leaves.

Farther ahead there was another black shape. He had started toward it when he realized that there were dark clumps everywhere he looked. Any of them could be Foxy. Or none.

The futility of what he was doing struck him. Nothing could be found in here that didn't want to be. Foxy was gone. He was never going to see her again.

He realized that he was crying. He didn't want to cry over a dog. But she might be hiding close by, afraid to show herself, dying when he could help her.

"Foxy! Trust me!"

Jeff's voice came out in a lonely wail that scared him. He felt cold and sick. He sat on a rock that jutted out of the water and covered his head with his arms.

The swamp seemed to wait until the sound of Jeff's cry died away. Then gradually, cautiously, it resumed its restless, secret life.

Chapter 27

Foxy, half-conscious in the wet leaves, heard Jeff's cry. Her ears flicked. Her head came up, wobbling unsteadily, and she listened.

Feelings stirred in her. Awareness came back, and with it discomfort and fear, but the sound she had heard meant safety.

She tried to get up; but her hind legs collapsed under her, and she fell sideward into the shallow water. Desperately she lurched upright and stood with her head hanging and her sides heaving. Then on quivering legs she staggered in the direction of Jeff's call.

He wasn't far away. When she saw him, she stopped dead. Her old fear of humans overwhelmed her, and she watched him intently, ready to run if he moved.

He was sitting with his back toward her, his arms hugging his legs, his head on his knees. Foxy was close enough to hear his breathing. As her fear lessened, she crept forward and crouched beside him, waiting to be noticed. She wanted to hear his voice again. She wanted to see his face. He didn't move, and she grew impatient. Gently, delicately she pushed her pointed muzzle up under his arm.

Jeff yelled and jumped to his feet. His reaction shocked Foxy. She backed away, but before she could run, he was on the ground with her, hugging her.

"I'm sorry, Foxy. You surprised me. Don't be afraid."

She squinted at him shyly, then suddenly flung herself on him, feverishly licking his face.

"Now don't start that," he said, but he didn't stop her. He pulled her onto his lap and held her tightly, rocking from side to side. "Foxy, Foxy," he said over and over.

Finally he stood up, and holding Foxy carefully in his arms, he began to slip and stumble out of the swamp. As they left the mangroves and started across the grass, Amber leaped from the car and ran wildly toward them.

"You found her!" she screamed, starting every dog in the kennel barking.

The whites of Foxy's eyes showed as she watched Amber's approach. "Don't worry about her, Fox," Jeff whispered. "Don't worry about anything. I'm going to protect you from the whole world."

"I told you! I told you!" Amber was shouting, but Foxy heard only Jeff. She wiggled around in his arms until her muzzle was on his shoulder and breathed a wet, contented sigh into his ear.

Chapter 28

It was a week before Foxy would come out of Jeff's tent without being dragged, two weeks before she could see Amber without trying to hide, three weeks before she could trot beside Jeff without cringing at every loud or sudden sound.

Campers weren't really supposed to have dogs, but Foxy was an exception. Within a day after Jeff had left the hospital, everyone in camp knew the story and kept Foxy in a state of quivering shyness with their friendly greetings and gifts of bones and scraps. They made a fuss over Jeff, too, feeding him and driving him to the hospital and giving him no chance to be lonely. Once he was sure his parents would be all right, Jeff began to have fun.

Now he stood looking around the stripped campsite, wondering how a month could have gone by so fast. This place had come to seem like home to him—the picnic table covered with drying towels; his shell collection scattered everywhere; the tent that smelled like Foxy whether or not she was in it. Messy but homey.

Now everything was stowed in the trailer, and his parents were in the rented car waiting for him; but he didn't want to leave. How could he go back to living indoors, sleeping in a bed, dressing for cold weather?

He walked to the edge of the water and stood there feeling the sun, hearing the gulls, watching the pelicans diving and diving. He wanted to store up the sight in his mind. By tomorrow he would be where there weren't any pelicans.

Something in the water looked interesting, an anemone maybe; but when he crouched to examine it, his father tapped the horn, and Jeff stood up reluctantly. He watched one more dive and then turned and walked slowly to the car.

He climbed into the backseat with Amber and Foxy, automatically protecting his face from Foxy's kisses.

"I wonder when she'll quit doing this," he said.

"Get used to it," Amber advised him.

Jeff's father started the car and drove slowly through the campground and out onto the road. They all were quiet. Jeff wanted to say something to lighten the mood, but he was afraid his voice would come out funny.

"Hard to leave, isn't it?" his mother said finally.

"I wish I were leaving," Amber grumbled.

Jeff's mother turned and smiled at her. "Maybe someday you can come to see us and Foxy."

Amber brightened. "When?"

"We'll see. I'll write to your mother."

They reached the highway, and Jeff's father pulled over. "Well, Amber, here's your stop."

Amber looked around at all of them. "Good-bye," she said in a subdued voice.

"Good-bye, Amber," Jeff's father said. "We'll always remember how good you and your parents were to Jeff through all this."

"That's okay," Amber mumbled.

"Kiss me good-bye, Amber," Jeff's mother said, and Amber leaned over the seat and flung her arms around her.

"Don't forget my visit," she said.

Jeff's mother laughed. "I won't forget."

"In the winter. I want to see snow."

"In the winter," Jeff's mother agreed.

Amber turned to Jeff. "Be sure and send me some of the pictures we took."

"Okay," Jeff promised.

"The one of you when you were still all bruised, and the one you took of me showing you how to dive, and the one of Foxy wearing flippers—"

"I'll get copies of the whole roll," Jeff said.

"Too bad we didn't get one of me driving the car."

Jeff flinched and glanced at his parents. How could Amber mention that? It was still a sore subject in his family, and he knew Amber had been in trouble over it. She'd been scared to death when King's barking woke her father and he caught them taking the car back. Now she didn't remember being scared. She thought of herself as a hero.

She took Foxy's muzzle between her palms and kissed her on the nose. "Good-bye," she said. "Come back when you get tired of Jeff."

Then she jumped from the car, and they watched her run across the highway to Dr. Gregg's kennel.

"It doesn't seem fair to make her work to pay that vet bill," Jeff's mother said. "After all, Foxy's our dog."

"She loves it," Jeff said unsympathetically. "She just complains because that's the way she is."

Jeff's father pulled back onto the highway, heading north, and Jeff watched the now-familiar landscape slip by. The swamps and thickets and glittering water didn't seem threatening to him anymore. He had had time to begin to understand the keys, to see how fragile they really were. They needed someone to protect them, he thought. The way Foxy did.

They were on the long bridge that Jeff had tried to walk across the night he thought Foxy was dying. It seemed a long time ago. Now Foxy was alert and healthy, but her early life had marked her. She would always be insecure and fearful. She would always need Jeff.

His father glanced over the back of the seat. "Look how Foxy's watching you," he said. "I wonder if she knows she's leaving her native state forever."

"It's my state, too," Jeff reminded him. He rubbed

Foxy's head roughly. "Don't be sad about leaving home, Fox. We'll be back someday."

Foxy squinted up at him and flopped her plumy tail against the seat.

"She's not sad," Jeff's mother said. "Wherever you are, that's home to Foxy."